"Cozy," De... settling himself beside her

With a little snort, Sam moved away from him, far more concerned than she should have been about his closeness. He smelled of the outdoors. She jerked away as his cold fingers touched her face.

"What's wrong?" he asked softly, his warm breath just brushing her cheek. "Why so touchy?"

"I'm not touchy. I just don't like the arrogant way you take control."

"Can it be the fair Selina is nervous of sharing this small dark space with a man? That she's been celibate too long?" he asked. "My touch seems to disturb you for some reason."

"Don't be ridiculous! I don't like you!"

"Oh, my poor innocent," Devlin taunted. "Liking has nothing to do with it."

EMMA RICHMOND says she's amiable, undomesticated and an incurable romantic. And, she adds, she has a very forbearing husband, three daughters and a dog of uncertain breed. They live in Kent. A great variety of jobs filled her earlier working years, and more recently she'd been secretary to the chairman of a group of companies. Now she devotes her entire day to writing, although she hasn't yet dispelled her family's illusions that she's reverting to the role of housekeeper and cook! Emma finds writing obsessive, time-consuming—and totally necessary to her well-being.

Books by Emma Richmond

HARLEQUIN PRESENTS
1203—TAKE AWAY THE PRIDE
1230—UNWILLING HEART
1317—HEART IN HIDING
1373—A TASTE OF HEAVEN

EMMA RICHMOND

law of possession

Harlequin Books

TORONTO • NEW YORK • LONDON
AMSTERDAM • PARIS • SYDNEY • HAMBURG
STOCKHOLM • ATHENS • TOKYO • MILAN

Harlequin Presents first edition December 1991
ISBN 0-373-11421-4

Original hardcover edition published in 1990
by Mills & Boon Limited

LAW OF POSSESSION

CHAPTER ONE

'WILL it be a white Christmas, Sam?'

'What? Oh, yes, darling, I expect so,' Sam murmured absently. God, where was he? She didn't think her overstretched nerves would stand much more. And how could she have been so stupid? she asked herself for the ninety-third time. She must have been insane! 'It seemed like a good idea at the time' would be written in blood on her grave.

Glancing at the clock, then at the dark window, the soft white flakes clearly visible, she sighed. She felt exhausted. Five, he'd said. I'll be there by five. It was now gone seven.

'Is he late, Sam?' Robbie asked worriedly, his dear little face set into anxious lines.

'Only a bit,' she murmured, trying to summon up a smile. 'I expect the trains were late or something.' Or he couldn't get a cab—or his car had broken down. In truth, she hadn't the faintest idea how he was travelling, she hadn't thought to ask him. Besides which, the public telephone in the post office hadn't exactly been the best place to conduct a private conversation, with half the village listening in. Walking across to where the small boy knelt on the window-seat, she ruffled his dark hair affectionately.

'But I can stay up till he comes? You promised, Sam,' he said urgently, forestalling her argument.

'Yes, I know, but that was because I expected he would be here by now,' she said wryly. 'Why not go and get into your pyjamas, hm?'

'Well, all right,' he agreed reluctantly. 'But if he comes, you will call me?'

'Yes, I'll call you. Go on, off you go.'

As he tore out of the room like a small tornado, Sam grimaced. A friend, she'd told Robbie. A friend is coming to visit—an occurrence so unusual as to merit intense excitement. Not many people came to visit—not her friends anyway. Her friends all lived in London and it was a little difficult for them to get to this God-forsaken place out on the Kent marshes. In summer, they said; promise, Sam, we'll come in the summer.

Hearing a car, she tensed, only to slump in limp relief when it went past. She hoped he didn't come, hoped he couldn't come. Not today; today, for some ridiculous reason, her nerves were shot to pieces. Tomorrow would be better, when she was calmer, more in control—and then there was the whisper of tyres on wet road, the muffled slam of a car door, and she felt sick. Yet she had loved him once, hadn't she? Had welcomed his visits? Until her stubbornness and his inflexibility had parted them, forever, she had thought. So why did he want to see her now? Had he had second thoughts? Or was he hoping that after he had left her to cope as best she might, she'd come round to his way of thinking? That seemed the most obvious reason. In which case she shouldn't have agreed to see him, because to see him, remember all they'd been to each other, would bring back the pain, the feeling of loss. Yet if he'd discovered he couldn't live without her . . .

Breaking her thoughts off midway, impatient with herself for asking questions that she couldn't possibly know the answers to until she'd spoken to him, Sam walked to the window and held the curtain aside, hoping, she supposed, that the sight of him would calm her, push away the stupid panic. Only it didn't, of course it didn't. How could it? Until she knew why he had come.

Taking a deep breath, she walked out into the hall. Switching on the porch light, she opened the front door, then simply stood there staring in shocked bewilderment, unable to comprehend what her eyes were telling her. Power, was her first impression, then arrogance. In his mid-thirties, his face very tanned, hard, his eyes curiously light—and she'd never seen him before in her life.

'Where's Paul?' she asked stupidly.

'What?' he demanded blankly, moving into the hall and dropping his heavy leather holdall with a thud at his feet.

'Paul,' she repeated. 'Paul Mason.' Then rapidly recovering her scattered wits, she demanded furiously, 'What the hell do you think you're doing? How dare you come in here without invitation?'

'Oh, I dare, lady, I dare,' he drawled—and then he smiled, very nastily, like a wolf.

'Get out,' she said tightly.

'No.'

'I'm not alone in the house,' she blustered. 'I only have to scream——'

'So scream,' he retorted indifferently as he began to shrug out of his anorak.

'I don't want to scream—and you can just put that back on again! You aren't staying!'

Ignoring her, he completed the removal of his coat and slung it towards one of the pegs along the wall. Standing in front of her, he waited. Sam also waited, her mouth tight, her eyes bright with fury.

'Just who the hell do you think you are?'

'I don't think, I know,' he returned with soft insolence. 'But I might ask you the same question— and with more reason.'

'What the devil is that supposed to mean?'

'It means, dear lady, that I'd like to know who you are.'

'Selina Anne Martin,' she said frostily. 'Now get the hell out of here!'

'Do I know you?'

'Of course you don't know me!' she yelled.

'Then it isn't much good telling me your name, is it?'

Staring at him, at this complete stranger, this large complete stranger, her mind insisted, who had casually invited himself inside, into her cottage, who stared at her with insolent eyes, behaved with such casual arrogance, Sam lost control. Grabbing his anorak, she thrust it violently against his chest. 'Get out!' she gritted. 'Pick up your bag and get out of my cottage!'

'Your cottage?' he asked softly.

'Yes! Mine!'

'Since when?'

'It doesn't matter since when!' she shouted. 'Now stop playing stupid games and go!'

'Got a copy of the lease, have you?' he asked with that nasty little inflexion that was grating very severely on nerves that had already been stretched to breaking-point.

'What?' she asked blankly.

'The lease,' he repeated coldly. 'Where is it?'

'In the bank!'

'Which bank?'

'It's none of your damned business! Now—Barclays in Rye,' she blurted as his face altered, became harder, menacing almost, making a mockery of her defiant courage.

'Well, you got that right at least.'

'Wonderful! I didn't know it was a quiz!'

'Neither did I when I came. Who did you buy the cottage from?' he asked silkily, the milder tone not at all deceiving her into thinking he wasn't angry, because he was. But why?

'I didn't buy it from anyone! Julie left it to——'

'Ah!' he exclaimed with a look of quiet satisfaction. 'Julie. And where, might I ask, is the delectable Julie now?'

'Dead,' Sam said bluntly, and was delighted to see the look of smug satisfaction wiped off his face, and then, while he stared at her, she began to use her brain instead of simply reacting. He'd fired his questions at her so fast, keeping her off balance, that she hadn't had a chance to consider the content. Just who the hell was this large man with the untidy brown hair that looked as though it had been bleached into stripes by the sun—at least, she assumed it was the sun; he certainly didn't look the type to go to the hairdresser's to have it streaked—and she suddenly felt an overwhelming desire to giggle.

'How long ago did she die?' he asked quietly.

'Three months ago—leukaemia,' she answered equally quietly, his question sobering her as no other could have done.

'I'm sorry,' he murmured, and she thought perhaps he might be—certainly the bright mocking eyes seemed to have softened. 'So who was Paul? Your lover?'

'No,' she denied automatically, then tightened her lips in exasperation. 'And even if he was, it's none of your damned business—and you still haven't explained what the hell you're doing here.'

'Haven't I?' he drawled, reverting to his earlier mockery. 'How remiss of me.' With a smile that was catlike in the extreme, he added softly, 'I, Miss Selina Anne Martin, am the landlord.'

'The land...' she began blankly. 'What do you mean, the landlord? Julie owned the cottage.'

'No, she didn't,' he denied in the same soft, hateful voice, shaking his head slightly to emphasise his words. 'I leased it to Julie for a term of five years. The fact that I returned home nearer six than five was a bonus for her, but the fact remains, Miss Martin, that I own the cottage. And now I've come home.'

'Home?' echoed Sam, her voice strangled.

'Home.'

'But you can't,' she said weakly. 'I live here.'

'No, Miss Martin. *I* do.' Slinging his anorak back on the peg, he picked up his bag, brushed past her and walked into the lounge.

Her mind whirling, Sam followed him and then just stood in the doorway staring helplessly at his broad back as he stood warming his hands at the fire.

'It can't be your cottage!' she exclaimed stupidly. 'Julie would have said——'

'It is my cottage, whether Julie said so or not,' he corrected flatly. 'And do I also gather that

another member of this charming family is shortly
to join us?' he asked without turning round.

'What?' she asked weakly.

'Paul—Mason, was it?'

'Paul?' Oh, hell, she'd forgotten all about Paul.
Groaning, she sank down on to the arm of the chair.
That was all she needed right now, for Paul to turn
up. Please God, she thought fervently, if you care
for me at all, don't let him come. 'No,' she
mumbled, 'he's not a member of the family. He's—
well, it doesn't matter what he is,' she added impatiently. Paul at the moment was the least of her
worries.

'Well, he must be pretty special—or you are,' he
murmured silkily, 'for him to venture out on a night
like this. But then even I, cynical devil that I am,
might even do so, for someone who looked like
you.'

'Don't even try,' she gritted. 'You wouldn't get
to first base.'

'But I am at first base,' he said softly, turning
to look at her, and the expression on his face made
her swallow drily and get hastily to her feet.

'Now look here, Mr whatever your name is...'

'Howe.'

'Howe,' she echoed stonily. 'You make one out-
of-place move, and I'll...' She'd what? If it was
his cottage, he must know as well as she did how
isolated they were. And with the fire flickering
behind him, the soft side lamp throwing eerie
shadows across his face, he looked dangerous. Her
eyes widening warily, Sam licked dry lips, then
wished she hadn't as his eyes followed the
movement. She was also unhappily aware of the
effect she had on men; how shouldn't she be?

Enough of them told her so. With a rather cynical smile that sat oddly on her beautiful face, she bravely held her ground. 'You lay just one finger on me, Mr Howe, or even look as though you're going to, and you'll regret it for the rest of your goddamned life!'

'Oh, oh, fighting talk,' he said softly, looking amused. 'Rest assured, Miss Martin, I have no intention of laying a finger on you, beautiful as you are, unless it's to bodily evict you. Hadn't you better start packing?'

'Sam?' Robbie called excitedly from the top of the stairs. 'Is it him?' and Sam's eyes widened in horror. Dear God, she'd forgotten all about Robbie waiting upstairs.

'No,' she said in a strangled voice, 'no.' Turning quickly, she began to run, hoping to intercept Robbie before he could rush in. Even a child as young as he couldn't fail to be aware of the fraught atmosphere in the small lounge. Only she had left it too late. In his usual energetic fashion, a beam of pleasure on his small face, he erupted through the doorway, nearly colliding with Sam on her way out. Wriggling past, he stared curiously at the tall man before the fire.

Don't, Sam pleaded silently. Don't diminish him, don't hurt him more, he thinks you're my friend—and that had to be the biggest joke of all time. This man would never be her friend. This man didn't look as though he had any friends.

'Hello,' Robbie said shyly, and Sam moved to put her hands protectively on Robbie's shoulders, then glared at this hard man who had come to disrupt their lives, begging—if glaring at him could by any remote stretch of the imagination be called begging—him not to say anything. Was there a softening in that cruel face, any trace of warmth in those hard, cynical eyes the colour of molten gold? They had a dark ring round the iris, she suddenly noticed, which gave him the look of a predator.

'This is Mr Howe, Robbie,' she said quietly, only the faintest tremor in her voice.

'Isn't it Paul?' he added in bewilderment.

'No, it doesn't look as though Paul is coming. Time for bed, I think. Say goodnight to Mr Howe.'

'Goodnight,' he said politely, then, grabbing Sam's hand in an almost desperate grip, he pleaded, 'Come and tuck me in, Sam?'

Nodding, she glanced briefly at the man standing before the fire, 'I won't be a moment,' she said quietly before leading Robbie from the room.

'Doesn't he like me, Sam?' Robbie asked worriedly as they went up the stairs.

'What? Oh, yes, of course, darling,' she comforted as she desperately forced herself to concentrate on Robbie's needs. 'I expect he's tired, maybe he had a long journey.' Presumably hell was quite a long way away. Dredging up a smile, and trying to appear relaxed, she tucked Robbie in and kissed him goodnight.

'Leave the door open, Sam.'

'I will,' she promised, as she promised every night.

Before re-entering the lounge, she took a deep steadying breath, wishing with all her heart that she didn't have to go in and face him, that she didn't have to beg.

'You shouldn't baby him,' he said flatly, not bothering to turn round from his contemplation of the snowy scene outside the window. 'He's old enough to take himself to bed.'

'In normal circumstances I might agree with you,' she said coldly, 'only the circumstances aren't normal. He's five years old, has recently lost his mother——'

'He isn't yours?' he asked in surprise.

'No, of course he isn't mine!' she said irritably. Having nerved herself to beg a few days' grace before being turfed out, she didn't want to be side-tracked. 'He's Julie's, and——'

'So Julie got married, did she? Well, well,' he murmured with the same sarcasm, 'she presumably overcame her aversion to the opposite sex...'

'What?' she asked, bewildered.

'Last time I saw her she informed me, quite bitterly, as I recall, that she would never get involved with another man as long as she lived!'

'Well, that's not surprising, is it?' she muttered rudely. 'If you were the last man she saw!'

With a cynically amused lift of one eyebrow that made Sam grind her teeth, he continued smoothly, 'So where's Daddy? Or can I expect him at any moment?'

Her mouth tight, her temper riding on a very taut rein, she gritted, 'I don't know where Daddy is. I don't even know who he was. Neither was Julie married——'

'My, oh, my,' he taunted, 'naughty Julie. She seemed so innocent too.'

'She was innocent,' she said through her teeth. 'Some bastard took advantage of her, then left her flat! And if, as you say, you rented this cottage to her, you must have known she wasn't the sort of girl to——'

'Sleep around?' he asked with hateful assistance when she came to a mumbled halt.

'She did not sleep around!'

'Oh, sorry—virgin birth, was it?'

'God, but you're hateful! As far as I'm aware,' Sam enunciated coldly, 'she slept with one man and one man only——'

'Then she must have known who the father was.'

'I didn't say she didn't! I said I didn't! And Robbie,' she added more quietly. It had been the only bone of contention between them, Sam insisting Robbie had a right to know and Julie obdurately refusing to tell him. Tell anyone, for that matter. Except the man's first name, she recalled bleakly.

'Tempt the gods and they extract payment,' he murmured wryly, then with a long sigh he ran one hand tiredly through his thick hair. 'Anyway, it's hardly my problem—or only in so far as getting the pair of you out of my home.'

'Well, you surely don't expect us to go tonight!' she exclaimed. 'Even you couldn't be that heartless!'

'What do you mean, even me? You don't know me. Don't know anything about me, so don't start throwing insults around, lady.'

'Why not?' Sam asked aggressively. 'You have, or do you think you have some sort of monopoly on it? I didn't know it was your home! I thought it belonged to Julie!'

'Well, it doesn't,' he denied flatly. 'However, even I,' he mimicked, 'can hardly turn a child out at this time of night. But tomorrow, Miss Martin, I want you both out! And don't,' he denigrated as she opened her mouth, 'trot out the trite old story of it being Christmas in a few days! I know it's Christmas in a few days!'

'And you still want us out! Yes, I get the picture! Perhaps you would also like to tell me where the hell we're supposed to go? The workhouse? That would seem to fit your notions pretty well.'

'Don't push me,' he said harshly, his eyes narrowed dangerously. 'It's not my fault your friend lied to you, and if I'd known she was going to use this place as a foundling home...'

'Don't be ridiculous! Julie was already pregnant when she came here.'

'Not when I saw her she wasn't! Or,' he added with a shrug, 'she must have only just become pregnant, because she was wearing very tight jeans when I saw her.'

'March,' she retorted.

'What?'

'I said March,' she repeated angrily. 'She must have conceived in March. Robbie was a full-term baby and he was born at the beginning of December. And before you start querying my brilliant arithmetic, I worked it out ages ago when I was trying to discover who the father might have been. What men Julie was likely to have known in March—and it came up zilch,' she added disgustedly. 'As far as I was aware, Julie had known no men in March. She was living with me then, while she looked around for somewhere to live, and she certainly didn't mention any men.' It had hurt, she remembered, transferring her gaze to the fire, that Julie had seemed unable to confide in her. 'Anyway,' she continued with an irritable sigh, 'that's neither here nor there. She had Robbie and she told me the cottage was hers!' Looking back at him, her face showing her defiance, she surprised a very odd look on his face. 'What?' she asked quietly.

'Nothing,' he muttered, turning away and staring out of the window again.

'Yes, it is,' she persisted. 'You looked—well, as though you might know something. Did she have a man with her when she came here?'

'No.'

'Then why did you look——'

'Leave it!' he gritted almost savagely. 'Just leave it!'

'How can I leave it? If you know something to do with Robbie's parentage, you have to tell me.' When he didn't answer, she walked across to him and grabbed his arm, then gasped in shock as he swung round and stared at her. His face was white, and her eyes widened in horrified comprehension. 'No,' she whispered. 'Oh, no.'

He stared at her, a nerve jumped in his jaw, then he shook his head as though to clear it. 'No, it can't be...'

'Did you...?' she began hesitantly.

'Yes, damn you!' he shouted. 'But we didn't——'

'What's your name?' she asked faintly.

'Devlin.'

'Devlin,' she echoed blankly. '"You're not to tell Devlin it's his"...'

'What?'

'That's what she said, when I insisted Robbie had a right to know: "Don't tell Devlin"...' Her eyes riveted on his face, wide and green, shocked. She could feel the tension in him, the rigid muscle beneath her hand, the stillness.

His eyes were fixed on hers, blind, then with a harsh bitter laugh he raked his hair back with both hands. 'Oh, wowee, instant fatherhood!' he exclaimed bitterly. 'Jesus wept! And for God's sake stop looking at me like that! I didn't know! Or am I now supposed to be overwhelmed with parental pride? The need to embrace him? Call him son? I don't want a son!' he bit out venomously.

'Then you shouldn't have got her pregnant! And, having got her pregnant, abandoned her!'

'I didn't abandon her, dammit! I didn't know she was pregnant!'

'Hah! Expect me to believe that?'

'I don't give a damn what you believe!' he grated, his face thrust close to hers. 'And how the hell could I have known she was pregnant when it was a one-night stand?'

Staring at him in outraged disbelief, incensed that he could lie so easily, denigrate her friend, Sam hit him. Her hand exploded against his face with a sound like a firecracker going off. 'Don't you dare besmirch her name like that!' she shouted. 'Don't you dare! I knew Julie, knew her from our prams, and she would never, ever behave like that!'

'Then you didn't know her as well as you thought,' he shouted back, 'because she sure as hell behaved like it that night. Or are you accusing me of rape?' he added softly, his eyes hard and brittle as glass, his jaw clenched as he fought to contain the anger that seemed likely to erupt from him at any moment.

'No,' she mumbled, suddenly frightened of where all this was leading, 'but Julie wasn't like that,' she repeated numbly. Never in her life had she met anyone who made her feel so unsure, so vulnerable, so overwhelmingly angry. Staring into his cold, arrogant face, she wondered at her courage. The red mark on his cheek was slowly turning white, and she felt a sick fear inside her for this man who looked as though violence was his middle name. Even tired as he obviously was, and shocked, power and energy seemed to radiate from every pore. And if he spoke the truth? No, her mind insisted, Julie wasn't like that, and to even think it for a moment was a betrayal. Then she gave an inward sigh of relief as he turned away. She wouldn't have been at all surprised if he'd hit her back.

'She was drunk,' he murmured almost inaudibly. With a half-laugh that wasn't in the least humorous, he muttered, 'So, for that matter, was I.'

'And that excuses it?' she asked in astonishment.

'No, it doesn't excuse it,' he denied irritably. 'Neither does it solve the problem of what to do about it.'

'Do about it?' echoed Sam, sudden fear darkening her eyes to jade. 'What do you mean, do about it?'

'What the hell do you think I mean?' he demanded as though she were mentally retarded. 'I have no room in my life for a child!'

'I didn't ask you to have room! I don't want you to have room! And even if I did, I wouldn't—which is just as well,' she added derisively to hide her apprehension, 'seeing that your reaction is no more than I would have expected. You don't have room, *ergo*, no child. Problem solved.'

'I didn't say that, dammit! And your sarcasm and holier-than-thou attitude I can well do without!'

'Yes, I just bet you can,' she retorted. 'Well, let me tell you——'

'No, Miss Martin, let me tell you,' he interrupted harshly. 'I am tired, hungry, I've been traveling non-stop for three days, and I cannot, and will not, bandy words about with you until I've had time to consider it, time to think. We'll discuss it in the morning.'

Opening her mouth to deny him the right of discussing it at all, she changed her mind. In truth she didn't think she could cope with another pointless argument either. 'I'll make some coffee,' she offered grudgingly.

'I'll make some coffee,' he mimicked, making Sam's mouth tighten again. Then with a sigh, he apologised, 'Sorry, coffee would be fine—and a sandwich if you have it. I seem to have missed some meals along the way...'

'Yes,' she said inadequately, 'and I don't find this any easier than you do, you know.' And wasn't that the truth?

'No, I don't suppose you do.'

'There's some stew I cooked for——'

'Paul,' he put in.

'Yes, for Paul.'

'And when I turned up instead, cold, hungry, tired, you took one look at me, decided you didn't like me, and the stew could go hang.'

'What did you expect?' she asked bitterly. 'You come pushing into the cottage, frightening me half to death... Oh, leave it!' she exclaimed tiredly. With a long sigh, she turned away and went out to the kitchen. Perhaps he would go, she thought hopefully, staring blankly at the kitchen wall. Perhaps he would just go, as abruptly as he'd come, then it would be all right, wouldn't it? She felt totally out of her depth, limp with reaction and exhaustion. Only why should he go? It was his damned cottage. Oh, Julie, she thought in despair, some legacy you left me with! And she found it so hard to comprehend that gentle Julie had made love with a man so—so lacking in feeling, so contemptuous of life. A man she barely knew. It was so unlike her. She'd never been one for going with boys, if anything she had been inclined to be prudish.

Rubbing a tired hand across her brow, too tired to even think any more, Sam walked across to the Aga and placed the saucepan of stew on the hotplate. Getting out two large soup plates and cutting thick slices from the loaf, she tried to shut her mind to Devlin Howe's disturbing presence. He took up too much room, she thought hazily, filled the tiny lounge with his presence, wrong-footed her, made her feel stupid, and she wasn't, not by any means.

'Need any help?' he asked quietly from behind her, making her jump violently. She hadn't even heard him come out.

'What?' she asked, swinging round to face him so that her dark chestnut hair swirled out around her face.

'I said——'

'I know what you said,' she muttered irritably, finding his presence too intrusive, too— overpowering.

'Well, then...'

'No—thank you,' she tacked on hastily, 'I can manage. Why don't you just sit down?' she added edgily.

'All right—but I think the stew's burning.'

Swivelling back to the stove, Sam cursed under her breath as she hastily removed the saucepan.

Go away, she pleaded silently. Move away from me and sit down, give me space, because if you don't, you're very likely to get the whole pan of stew thrown at you. She felt as though she were about to explode, her insides jangling and twisting together.

'Shall I set the table?'

'If you wish,' she said stiffly. 'Cutlery's in the drawer next to the sink.'

Spooning stew into the bowls with a hand that shook, she carried them to the table, then put the basket of bread in the middle before putting the coffee on to percolate.

Seating herself opposite him, she kept her eyes on her plate, wondering how on earth she was going to eat. Her throat felt blocked tight, and he didn't seem to be faring any better. He only took a few mouthfuls before he began pushing the stew irritably back and forth across the dish.

'God, what a mess!' he exclaimed suddenly, throwing down his spoon. 'Once. Just once, one night, one disastrous bloody night!' Pushing his chair back with a violent movement that made the legs scrape on the tiled floor, he got to his feet and stalked into the lounge.

Her hands clenched on the table, Sam stared blindly into the cooling stew. Oh, God. She couldn't cope with this man with his violent changes of mood, she really couldn't. Couldn't come to terms with the fact that he was Robbie's father. Robbie's father, for goodness' sake! Pushing her plate away, she got agitatedly to her feet. Pouring out two mugs of coffee, she carried them into the lounge and put them on the low coffee-table.

'I didn't know if you took sugar,' she mumbled inanely. 'I put in two,' but she didn't think he even heard. He was standing at the window again, his hands shoved into his jeans pockets. Strong legs, she thought inconsequentially, powerful thighs, broad shoulders. The muscles in his neck and back were taut and she felt the violence in him, the frustration, and against her will she began to feel a shred of pity. A long, tiring journey, looking forward to relaxing, catching up on his sleep, and what does he find? His cottage occupied by a strange woman, and that he's the father of the child with her—and she just wished, she thought wrathfully, that she could rid herself of this irritating habit of always seeing everyone else's point of view! She might feel pity, but she could never forgive him for what he'd done to Julie.

'I'd already had too much to drink when she arrived that night, the night before I left,' he began quietly, almost as though he were talking to himself. 'I opened the door to her, whisky bottle in one hand, glass in the other—I'd been trying to drink myself under the table, the reasons for which aren't important, and there was Julie—someone else putting on a brave face. Eyes too bright, voice too loud. She'd come a day early, she explained, and was it all right? Sure, I said, what the hell? Could she have some of what I was drinking, she thought she needed it? And like lost souls, we emptied the bottle between us. I don't know what her trouble was, some man perhaps, or her mother. I vaguely recall her saying something about her mother...' and Sam nodded in agreement. Julie and her mother had practically destroyed each other, rows, arguments that gentle Julie could never cope with.

'...something like that, anyway,' he continued reminiscently. 'To be honest, I don't remember very much, most of it's just a blur—and presumably going to bed together must have seemed like a good idea at the time. In the morning, when I woke, there she was, and for the life of me I couldn't even remember how she'd got there. Face smudged with mascara, hair a tangled mess—she looked lost and lonely and vulnerable.'

'And you felt like the biggest heel of all time,' Sam put in softly, unaware that she was about to say it until she did so. But that was the truth of it, she knew. She could see the whole scene, and that made everything ten times worse. His look of astonishment didn't help much either.

'From someone you took an instant dislike to, you're being very understanding.'

'It was the way you said it,' she explained simply, her voice soft, her extraordinary green eyes fixed on his. 'Brutally, glaringly—honestly. You look like a man who's had to fight every inch of his way through life, tough, uncompromising—you don't strike me as the sort of man who would enjoy hurting someone who couldn't fight their way out of a paper bag.' And that was true too. She should have known the moment she saw him that he wouldn't have left Julie knowing she was pregnant. There was a defiant sort of honesty about him, a sort of damn-it-to-hell, take-it-or-leave-it attitude. Not that it excused him, but she could understand. 'Besides,' she continued, feeling compelled to at least partly exonerate him, 'I'd known Julie a long time, I know the effect she had on people. One look of gentle reproof, one sad smile, and you'd feel one of the worst human beings ever created, and if you were both drunk, reasoning processes shot to pieces, and she wanted comfort, or you did...'

'Yes. Big sad eyes, like a damned puppy, not that that's any excuse. And she apologised,' he whispered, sounding agonised. 'Sorry, she said, as though it had all been her fault. I felt like a grubby schoolboy. She washed and dressed, smiled, apologised again, helped me load up my car. I wrote out my name and an address where I could be contacted in case there were any problems. Neither of us had taken any precautions—well, you don't when you're drunk, do you?' he asked bitterly. 'I said something trite about her enjoying her stay in the cottage, not to seduce the local farmers, and she said not to worry, she was off men. I never heard from her, or saw her again.'

'No,' murmured Sam, and that was presumably why Julie would never tell her who the father had been. Because she took the blame, lay the fault at her own door. Don't tell Devlin. And Sam hadn't been able to, because she hadn't known who he was. Yet Julie had known he would come back, would find Sam here with Robbie... Or did she? Julie had been expecting her to marry Paul. She hadn't told Julie that Paul had flatly refused to look after her son. And presumably if she had married Paul, had put the cottage on the market, she'd have found out that it wasn't hers to sell... Only none of that had happened, because she hadn't married Paul. Oh, Julie, she thought helplessly, what a mess! Taking a long, shaky breath, she stared back at Devlin Howe. 'I'm sorry,' she apologised quietly. 'I thought...'

'I know what you thought, you made your opinions very plain.'

'Yes, but that doesn't excuse what happened, that you couldn't control——'

'No,' he said coldly, cutting her off. 'So where do we go from here?'

'We don't go anywhere. She obviously never intended for you to know...'

'But she knew I'd be back. What in God's name did she think I'd do when I found you and a small boy in my cottage?'

'I don't think she did expect it—that I'd still be here, I mean...'

'You said she left you the cottage!' he grated impatiently.

'Yes, but—oh, I don't know!' Sam exclaimed wearily. 'I can't think straight. If I'd have known in advance who you were, I wouldn't have told you——'

'But you didn't! And I do know!' he denigrated shortly. 'So what happens now?'

'I don't know, do I?'

'Well, what do you want to happen?' he demanded aggressively.

'Me?' she asked in surprise. 'I want you to go away and not come back!' she retorted agitatedly. 'Only you won't, will you?'

'No.'

'So I'd best set about making other arrangements, hadn't I? No,' she added hastily, seeing by the expression on his face that he was about to offer money, maintenance. 'Oh, no. You said yourself you have no room in your life for a child, didn't want encumbrances. Julie made me Robbie's guardian, and once we've found somewhere to live, we'll be fine.'

'Will you?' he taunted, going across to sit on the edge of the sofa facing her. 'And for how long will you be fine? You're what? Twenty-four, -five?' and when she nodded, he continued inexorably, 'and Robbie's just started school——'

'No, he doesn't start until after Easter.'

'Don't split hairs,' he derided impatiently. 'That still leaves thirteen years to go before he could reasonably be expected to leave home, thirteen years of responsibility, staying in, no career, making ends meet.'

'Not necessarily,' she said stiffly. 'And if I hadn't wanted the responsibility, I wouldn't have taken it on.'

'Wouldn't you? When Julie pleaded with you? Big sad eyes at their most anguished? Ah, hit a nerve, didn't I? Do you have a family?' and when she nodded, he asked, 'And what did they say?'

Tempted to lie, Sam made the mistake of looking at him, and was forced into honesty. Those cat's eyes of his seemed to stare into her soul and see the truth. 'Much as you've done,' she muttered. 'But do you think I could have slept nights if I hadn't taken him? Had him put into care?'

'What about Julie's parents? Wouldn't they have taken him?'

'You must be joking! Her father died some time ago, and her mother certainly didn't want him, she thought Julie should have had an abortion—anyway, she remarried recently. I don't even know where she lives. Certainly she never showed any desire to see her grandson,' she muttered, her voice reflecting the anger she still felt at Julie's mother's indifference.

'And how do you manage for money? This is hardly a thriving community, unless it's changed radically in the last few years. All I remember of the place were a few scattered cottages and some bedraggled-looking sheep.'

'No, it hasn't changed, but I manage,' she said firmly, which was a complete and utter lie; still, she wasn't about to tell him that. 'I rented out my London flat to an American for six months; it pays the mortgage on it and leaves a little over. I do the accounts of a local farmer, a bit of typing for an author in the village. Besides, once Robbie's over the worst of it, I shall probably move back to London. I can work while he's at school. I didn't want to move too soon—I thought it might be harmful to take him away from all he's ever known.'

'I see. And men, marriage?'

'That, Mr Howe, is none of your business!' Getting to her feet, she took her empty coffee-mug out to the kitchen and made a great performance of clearing the uneaten stew away.

'Another nerve?' he asked softly.

Slamming the plates down, Sam whirled to face him. 'I will accept,' she began icily, 'that you have a possible right to probe into Robbie's welfare, even though you have only this minute discovered he's your son. What you do not have the right to do is probe into my private life! What I do about men or marriage is my affair, not yours!'

'It is if it affects Robbie,' he said softly. 'Suppose you meet someone, someone who's prepared to take on Robbie? I might not like him, might not think he's suitable . . .'

'You might not think . . .' she floundered. Taking a deep breath in an effort to hold her fiery temper in check, she grated, 'Then tough! An accident of birth does not make you responsible for either of us. By law, I'm Robbie's guardian, not you. Your name doesn't even appear on the birth certificate——' Then she broke off, mortified, as he went white. 'I'm sorry,' she whispered, 'that was below the belt—but I've no intention of allowing you to interfere in my life. I have no objection to your seeing Robbie now and again to make sure he's all right, but anything else, no. You must see what an intolerable intrusion into my privacy I'd find it.'

'And you must see that I can't just walk away. Whatever the rights or wrongs, I do know about him.' Running a hand through his shaggy hair, he sighed, long and deeply. 'God, I'm too tired for this, we're just going round in circles. I'd better try and get a room in Rye . . .'

'Yes, you could take my car. For obvious reasons, I can't take you myself.'

'Why would I need to take your car? I can ring for a cab.'

'I don't have a phone.'

'Don't have a phone?' he exclaimed. 'Why not? There was one here when I left.'

'I know, I know,' she said irritably. 'Julie had it taken out. She said she liked being isolated, cut off.'

'Well, that was damned irresponsible, wasn't it, when she had a child to consider? What happened if there was an accident? An emergency——?' Breaking off, he gave a depressed sigh. 'I suppose she couldn't afford it.'

'Of course she could! She was a potter, a very good craftswoman, and certainly she made enough to be able to afford a phone.'

'Then how the hell did she take orders if she couldn't communicate with anyone?'

'She dealt direct with a craft shop in Rye. Each time she took a batch in, they'd give her orders for the next lot. There's a shed and kiln at the bottom of the garden,' Sam added as though that explained everything. In truth, like him, she was too tired to think coherently. 'I never bothered to have it re-installed, because—well, because I didn't expect to be here very long. Oh, I'll make you up a bed on the sofa!' she exclaimed impatiently, otherwise she could see them discussing it until the small hours. Brushing past him, she went upstairs to get some blankets.

She didn't even know if he had a family of his own; didn't know what he did, didn't know anything except that he continually wrong-footed her, made her angry. Her arms full of bedding, she returned to the lounge and began to make up the sofa. Smoothing the top blanket with a nervous gesture, aware that he was watching every move she made, she finally straightened and turned to face him, her chin tilted defiantly. He was leaning against the wall, arms folded, eyes fixed on her, a brooding expression on his strong face.

'Are you married?' she asked bluntly. 'Could this cause complications?'

'No.'

'Engaged?'

'No, Miss Martin, neither am I engaged—just loosely attached, one might say. Fortunate, isn't it?' he asked with hateful sarcasm.

'Yes.'

'Just like your circumstances,' he said, rather tauntingly, she felt.

'Yes,' she agreed stiffly.

'So who was he?' he persisted, his eyes narrowed on her face. 'Someone who wouldn't take on Robbie?'

Refusing to answer, Sam made a great performance of brushing pieces of blanket fluff from her sweater, before saying quietly, 'If there's anything you want, please help yourself. I'll leave you to get some sleep.' As she went to walk past him, he caught her arm in a punishing grip.

'You have little brown flecks in your eyes,' he murmured, then gripped her chin hard when she tried to look away. 'Selina,' he said softly.

'Sam,' she corrected. 'Everyone calls me Sam.'

'Sam,' he echoed. 'A masculine name for a very feminine lady.'

'Please let me go,' she whispered, tension locking her muscles rigid. She didn't like that predatory gleam in his eye, nor the feel of his callused fingers that seemed to burn her skin, and she was suddenly frightened, not only of him, but of the confusion he seemed to arouse in herself.

'Is that what he said to you?' he asked coolly. 'Please let me go? What a fool to let something so exquisite slip through his fingers.'

Flicking startled eyes back to his, she flushed, and the most awful warmth seemed to spread inside her at the expression in those golden eyes.

'Skin like buttermilk, isn't that what they say? Eyes like emeralds, and hair like burnished copper—no, polished chestnuts. See? Poetry in the soul of the hardest man. A woman a man might think the world well lost for—only obviously he didn't, because he didn't come, did he?' Tossing her arm away from him in a gesture that was almost insulting, he added with amused contempt, 'Goodnight, Sam—we'll talk tomorrow.' With a mocking little bow, he walked across the room and held the door open for her.

CHAPTER TWO

HER mouth tight, Sam hastily escaped. What the hell right did Devlin Howe have to be contemptuous of her? There were probably half a dozen excellent reasons why Paul hadn't come, she thought defiantly as she hurried up the stairs. Roads blocked, trains not running—yet Devlin Howe had managed. Furious with herself for even caring what that hateful, arrogant man had said, she hurried into her room. With no central heating in the cottage, the bedroom was like an ice-box, and she hastily shrugged out of her clothes and into her dressing-gown. Dashing along to the bathroom, terrified almost that Devlin might come up before she was safely in bed, she had a sketchy wash before scurrying back to her room. Whipping her nightdress over her head, she huddled beneath the blankets, her teeth chattering.

The covers clutched to her chin, she stared at the window, watching the white flakes that drifted against the glass. Devlin Howe. Over and over her mind whispered his name. Robbie's father. So much to assimilate, so much to come to terms with, and against her will her mind persisted in conjuring up images of that hard, tanned body, beside Julie. That sneering mouth, kissing her, his hands touching her... With a snarl of impatience and disgust, she turned over and thumped the pillow. How could Julie have let him? Easily, her mind whispered. Whatever else he was, he was all man. A damned attractive man, but one thing she was very determined on: he wasn't going to screw up her life! No way was he going to interfere with her upbringing of Robbie! He had no rights, and pity or compassion or whatever would not make her agree to his having any! And if when he'd spent the night thinking about it and come up with some highfalutin solutions, she would make that very plain! Julie had left Robbie to her, and, whatever the rights and wrongs of her friend's decision, Devlin bloody Howe was not going to overset them! She loved Robbie as if he were her own, and she would fight tooth and nail to keep him!

Yet where were they to go? Despite her fine words to Devlin, her finances were shaky—very, very shaky. That old woman Parsons, the bank manager, was getting decidedly picky! Only how the hell was she supposed to stay in credit when her outgoings were more than her incomings? It would be all right, it would possibly be all right, she mentally corrected, when they returned to London, but until then... She couldn't afford to rent anything, couldn't afford to do anything! Worried sick, she tried to think of a bright idea for making money. Any idea—or any idea that didn't involve Devlin Howe. She was damned if she would allow herself to become his charity case! Only why in heaven's name hadn't Julie told her?

It was a long time before she fell asleep, and even then it wasn't a deep or refreshing sleep, and it seemed barely moments after she'd closed her eyes before she was woken by the excited voice of her ward.

'Sam! Sam! Look!'

Groaning and trying to hang on to the covers that Robbie was determinedly dragging off her, Sam opened her eyes. The room was too bright, she decided, and it took her a moment or two to realise why. Glancing across to the window, she saw an unending vista of white. Oh, no! Scrambling out of bed, shivering as her feet touched the cold floor, she gazed in disbelief at the snow-covered landscape. Not just a dusting as she might have expected after last night's snowstorm, but deep, high drifts that covered the shed at the end of the garden, piled against the fences. Rushing across the landing and into Robbie's room, Sam stared out at the road. Road? It was impossible to see where the road was, only the line of telegraph poles marching off into the distance bore any resemblance to normality. Peering downwards, she stared at the white hump that was her car. And just to make everything perfect, a large snowflake drifted past the window, rapidly followed by others. Terrific. She would never get her car along roads that deep in snow, neither would anyone else be able to get in, until the snow-ploughs came, and this isolated little community would hardly be number one on the council's list of priorities. Yet today was the day Devlin Howe had told her she must leave. And if they couldn't? Then they would be stuck here with him—and that wasn't a thought that brought any comfort! Remembering all that had occurred the previous evening, Sam gave a despondent sigh. It also presumably meant that Paul wouldn't be able to come. Although maybe that was as well. She had the horrible feeling that Paul and Devlin wouldn't get on too well. Don't lie, Sam, she chided herself, you know damned well Paul and Devlin wouldn't

get on. It would be like asking the hawk and the
eagle not to fight. But at least Paul would present
an opportunity to escape. She could throw herself
on his mercy... Oh, very funny, Sam. Yet it
shouldn't have been funny. If he'd really loved her,
he would have given herself and Robbie sanctuary
for a few days while she decided what to do.

'Don't you like snow, Sam?' asked Robbie,
putting a comforting arm round her legs.

'Sure, I think it's wonderful,' she muttered
gloomily as she gazed at the transformed landscape.

'Can I go out? Can I, Sam? Make a snowman?'

'Not in your pyjamas, no,' she said drily, turning
and forcing herself to smile down at him. 'Most
certainly not in your pyjamas.' And what's going
to happen to you, my little lad? she wondered unhappily. You don't know the half of it.

When Robbie giggled and ran over to his cupboard to drag his clothes out, she returned her gaze
to the snow-covered fields. Oh hell! She'd been
going to get the Christmas tree today, and the
turkey, and the rest of Robbie's presents. Only what
was the point in getting a Christmas tree if you
didn't have a home to put it in?

'Is it a problem?' Devlin asked quietly from the
doorway, and she turned, startled. Did the damned
man creep everywhere? He was dressed in a heavy-
knit navy sweater and close-fitting jeans—and he'd
shaved, she noticed... and seemed far more disturbing than he had the night before. His eyes
looked more amber in daylight, his hair darker.

'Problem?' she asked with a bitter little laugh.
'Why should it be a problem? I can probably con-
struct a sled to transport our belongings; build an

igloo for Robbie and myself to live in until the snow melts.' Returning her gaze to the window, she stared blindly out. She didn't want to look at him, she found. Didn't want to accept that they were going to have to stay here with him, whether he liked it or not. Didn't want to be disturbed by him.

'Don't you like snow, Sam?' he taunted, proving that he'd been eavesdropping on her conversation with Robbie. He also sounded as though he was smiling, and she found that disturbing too.

'Sure,' she mumbled, glancing irritably at him over her shoulder, 'it's terrific. I couldn't have asked for anything nicer. And unless you really do intend me to build an igloo, or presumably live in the shed, you do realise what this means, don't you?'

'Oh, yes, Sam, I realise exactly what it means,' he concurred as he leaned indolently against the door-frame. 'Igloos aside, it means you either have a very long walk to get to Rye and find a hotel, maybe get lost, contract frostbite—or it means we all stay cosily at the cottage until it thaws.'

'Yes. It doesn't seem to bother you,' she muttered aggrievedly.

'No, why should it? I've been living in Canada— they have a lot of snow there. I guess you could say I'm used to it.' Which wasn't precisely what she'd meant, as he very well knew. 'I've made the tea,' he added, a rather disruptive gleam of amusement in his eyes.

'Thank you. I'll be down directly—Robbie, you have your boots on the wrong feet,' she added peevishly, then watched rather crossly as Devlin lowered his long length to the floor and gently removed the boots and pushed them on to the right feet. Why was he being so damned accommodating all of a sudden?

'You'll need a thick jumper, warm coat, hat, gloves,' he said softly, and Robbie grinned up at him, obviously relieved that his remoteness of the night before was gone.

They didn't look very much alike, Sam thought absently as she stared at them, the two heads so close together. In fact they didn't resemble each other at all. Suddenly aware that Devlin was watching her, she raised her eyebrows haughtily.

'Yes?'

'Oh, nothing. I just wondered if I ought to mention the fact that I can see straight through your nightdress. I wouldn't want to be accused of——'

Only Sam had heard enough. With a startled exclamation, she hurried out and into her room, slamming the door behind her. Hastily opening it again, she yelled across the landing, 'Robbie! You're not to go out without any breakfast!'

Damn him! Collecting her robe and clean underwear, she hastened along to the freezing bathroom where she had a quick wash and cleaned her teeth before dashing back to her bedroom. Dressing swiftly in thick socks, jeans and a warm sweater, she went reluctantly downstairs.

A pot of porridge was bubbling on the Aga, and Robbie was already seated at the table tucking into a bowlful. Cups and saucers were set out, the teapot steaming beneath the red wool cosy. Devlin was leaning rather nonchalantly back against the sink. He looked amused. Glaring at him, Sam sat at the table and poured herself some tea, then muttered a grudging thank-you as he ladled her out some porridge and set it in front of her. Neither spoke until Robbie had struggled into his anorak, mittens and woolly hat and dived out of the back door with a yell of delight.

Closing the door after him, Devlin came to sit opposite her.

'What can't be cured must be endured,' he taunted softly as he poured his own tea. 'Stop sulking. We have more important things to worry about than our personal feelings, like provisions, logs...'

Staring at him, wishing she could refute his logic, Sam looked away when a gleam of wicked mockery entered his eyes. She would like to know what had changed his attitude so abruptly. Last night he'd been abrasive, sarcastic, angry. This morning he was mockingly amused, as though it were a game.

'Don't you even care?' she burst out.

'About what?'

'Robbie! Julie! Everything!'

His eyes narrowing dangerously, he said softly, 'Leave it. I said leave it, Sam,' he repeated when she opened her mouth to argue, then nodded approvingly when she shut her mouth with a snap. 'So?' he prompted. 'What are the priorities?'

Glaring at him, her face pinched and white, dark circles under her eyes from lack of sleep, she forced her temper under control. When she thought she could actually speak without her voice cracking, she said quietly, 'We'd maybe better make a list. I'll get a pad and pencil.' Getting abruptly to her feet, she walked into the lounge. She was shaking, and felt she was about to come apart at the seams. Detestable, hateful, arrogant man! He was probably one of those infuriating people who were always right—or thought they were! He'd lit the fire, she

saw, yet she found it very hard to summon up any
gratitude. She would rather have hypothermia than
have him in the cottage; then she felt a wave of
guilt wash over her. He'd made the tea, fed Robbie,
and had more right than she to be here. It was his
cottage, after all. Only it didn't feel like his cottage.
It felt like hers! Collecting a pad and a pen from
the pot on the mantelpiece, she went back to the
kitchen and resumed her place opposite him.

'I'm sorry,' she apologised stiltedly, giving him
a small conciliatory smile that was little more than
a token gesture. 'You're right, of course. We have
to make the best of things.'

'And there's nothing more infuriating than
people being right, is there?' he queried, his face
straight.

'No,' she agreed stiffly, fighting the desire to
throw the pad at him. Opening it in a businesslike
fashion, she held the pen poised. 'We'll need more
wood for the fire and the stove—thank you for
lighting the fire, by the way.'

'A small return for your—er—hospitality,' murmured Devlin.

Mortified that she had so quickly forgotten who
owned what, Sam pushed the pad towards him. 'I'm
sorry, I keep forgetting it's your cottage. Perhaps
you'd like to make the list.'

'Shut up,' he said without emphasis, pushing the
pad back. 'How's the food situation?'

'That's OK. By a stroke of good luck I filled the
freezer yesterday—and I'm sure Robbie won't mind
having chicken rather than turkey for Christmas
dinner. I've still got some candles from when we
had the bad storms last month—just in case the

electricity goes,' she explained aloofly when Devlin looked astonished.

'Ah yes, I'd forgotten England's good old inefficiency.'

Tempted to tell him he should have stayed away if he didn't like it, Sam bit her lip. There was no need to make things worse than they already were. He appeared to be trying to be friendly, the least she could do was reciprocate; it was only for a few days, after all. 'From your tone I assume Canadians are always prepared for snow and don't have to make do and mend until the local council, and the electricity board, get their respective fingers out! If the cables come down with the weight of snow, it could be days before we're reconnected. Which of course you'll know. Now, what else?' she continued hastily at his look of dry mockery. 'I can collect some branches to decorate instead of a tree...'

'So the real problem is logs?' he asked.

'Yes. I was due a delivery today.' Allowing her glance to drift past him to the window, Sam saw that the snow seemed to be falling heavier than ever, and she grimaced. 'We're not exactly inundated with trees around here. Also I'll need to try and get to the Forresters...'

'My God, are they still here? I'd have thought they'd have died years ago.'

'Well, they didn't,' she said crossly, 'so we'll have to check that they're OK.'

'We?' he enquired, amused. 'A moment ago it was I.'

'All right, I'll go and check they're all right. From there I'll go on to the Gunners——'

'Gunners?' he queried, puzzled.

'David and Barbara Gunner. They live at Grantham Farm.'

'What happened to old Ted Akers? Died?'

'No, he went to live with his daughter in Bristol,' she explained impatiently. 'David took over about a year ago.'

'Well, whatever so, the Gunners—are they elderly too?'

'No, and they should be all right—they're fairly young with a small boy, Peter, who's a little older than Robbie, but it might be as well to check if we can——' Then Sam smiled as she heard a dog barking excitedly. 'Sounds as if we've been pre-empted. That sounds like Brandy, David's dog.'

Getting to her feet, her face wreathed in a warm, natural smile that made her look not merely lovely, but quite extraordinarily beautiful, she was un-aware that Devlin stared at her speculatively as she opened the back door. 'You look like the abomin-able snowman,' she teased, lightly brushing snow from David's dark hair. 'Come in,' she added warmly. Seeing where his glance was resting, she looked awkward for a moment and was inordi-nately grateful when Devlin took command.

'Devlin Howe,' he said easily, getting to his feet. 'I'm a friend of Sam's. I called in yesterday to see if she was all right and got caught by the storm.'

'Which was probably a blessing,' answered David, giving Sam a small smile. David, bless him, was totally incapable of reading nuances into any conversation and would, she knew, accept Devlin's words at face-value. Extending his hand to the other man, he added, 'Barbara sent me over to invite Sam to share Christmas with us—but I can see now that won't be necessary. You won't be able to leave for days, and Sam won't want to leave you on your own. Although,' he added after a frowning pause, 'you'd be very welcome to come as well.'

'No, that's all right, thanks very much anyway. But we'll be fine.'

Giving Devlin a look behind David's back that said quite clearly that they wouldn't be fine at all, and that, far from being reluctant to leave him on his own, she'd be more than delighted, she could have hit him, when he smiled nastily back.

'Now,' David continued, unaware of the little byplay, 'how are you off for food? Barb's spent the evening baking, so I brought over some bread—and fresh milk and eggs.'

'Thank you, that's kind,' praised Sam, trying to inject warmth into her tone before even David began to wonder what on earth was going on, 'but I'm OK for food, I stocked up yesterday. All we seem to be short of is wood for the fires.'

'Mm, me too—I was just about to go foraging—and two more strong arms will be a great help,' David continued with a glance at Devlin. 'Between us, we should manage OK.'

'Fine, I'll go and get my boots,' Devlin replied, his eyes still full of hateful amusement. Getting to his feet, he went out, and David grinned in approval. In the country everyone helped everyone else, something Devlin obviously knew, although Sam didn't know how long he'd lived here before he went away, but if Devlin hadn't offered, David's estimation would have gone down very severely, and Sam wasn't quite sure whether she was pleased or sorry that it hadn't.

'The Forresters have gone to relatives for Christmas,' David continued blithely, unaware of

Sam's thoughts, 'so we needn't worry about them. Now, anything else?'

'No, I don't think so—thanks, David. We were just about to come and see if you were all right.' She smiled.

Accepting the cup of tea she poured for him, he remarked seemingly idly. 'Seems like a nice chap—known him long?'

'Not long, no,' she admitted cautiously.

'Mind my own business, mm?' he asked with a grin, obviously misunderstanding her reticence.

'Is there anything Barbara needs?' she asked, adroitly changing the subject. If David thought she and Devlin were romantically involved, it didn't matter, did it? Well, it wouldn't have to, she thought impatiently, because she had no intention of explaining. She could just imagine how that bit of information would be received in the village.

'No, only to know that you were OK—and to ask if you wanted to unload Robbie for a few hours to play with my horror. I'd bring him back before it gets dark.'

'Oh, he'd like that,' Sam said gratefully. 'Also, could you take Peter's Christmas presents? Only a few little things to go under the tree,' she explained with an embarrassed smile as she bent to pick up the carrier bag full of little gifts she'd wrapped the day before. She hadn't been able to afford much, but David and Barbara had been so kind to her since Julie died that she wanted to repay them even if only in a small way.

'Daft girl, spending your money on my monster, but thank you,' David mumbled, sounding as embarrassed as she felt. Bending, he gave her a swift kiss on the cheek just as Devlin returned. 'I'll see you about four,' he said softly, 'and I see your man's ready,' he added, glancing at Devlin, 'so we'll be off.' With another smile, he left, and she heard him shouting to Robbie to get on the sledge.

'Another man in your pocket, Sam?' Devlin asked insinuatingly.

'No,' she denied between her teeth, 'and even if it was, it's no business of yours.'

'Only of his wife's?'

'That's right.' Holding his stare, her eyes wide and determinedly innocent, she gave a little sigh of relief when he turned away. And put that in your pipe and smoke it, Devlin Howe! She couldn't care less if he thought her some sort of Delilah. So long as he didn't think he could enter the lists!

'You'll be all right?' he asked quietly and with quite spurious concern.

'Of course. I have lots of things to do—if that's all right,' Sam added belatedly. Oh, it was so difficult to remember she had no right to make free of the cottage.

'The only thing that isn't all right,' he said with a touch of asperity, 'is you apologising every five minutes. Of course it's all right! What the hell did you expect? That I'd throw you out in the snow?'

'Yes. No, of course not,' she contradicted herself awkwardly as she watched him shrug into his anorak, not entirely sure that she believed any such thing. 'Take care, won't you?'

'Care that I do fall into a snow-drift, or don't?' he asked smoothly.

'Do,' she said under her breath as he closed the door after him. Watching until they were out of sight, she sighed, then turned away to clear the table. How on earth were they going to co-exist for

the next few days without coming to blows? And
without Robbie noticing the strained atmosphere?
She could try being a bit more friendly, she supposed moodily as she ran hot water into the sink.
If she made a very special effort not to lose her
temper. Oh yeah? she derided, her mouth twisting.
And since when have you ever been meek? Someone
only has to say one word out of place and you go
up like a rocket on November the fifth! If it had
been someone like David, there wouldn't have been
a problem. Only it wasn't someone like David...
Oh, to hell with it, she thought impatiently. As he'd
said, what can't be cured must be endured.
Throwing the washing up cloth at the wall to relieve
her churning feelings, she dried up and put everything neatly away.

She spent the next few hours giving the cottage a
thorough clean, setting up the old camp-bed in
Robbie's room, making up the fire and wrapping
Robbie's presents. She iced the cake which she'd
made a few days before, then surveyed the rather
wobbly writing with a rueful smile. Hardly profes-
sional, but she didn't suppose Robbie would mind.

Feeling better, calmer, after her burst of energy,
she determined that despite the lack of tree and
turkey, and the fact that as soon as the snow thawed
they would be homeless, she was going to make this
a special Christmas for Robbie, the first without
his mother—which meant trying to get along with
Devlin Howe. That wasn't so hard, was it? Wasn't
it? she asked herself wryly. Personally she thought
it would be well-nigh impossible. But she promised
herself she would try. Hard.

She was up in the loft when Devlin returned, looking for the Christmas decorations. 'I'm up here!' she called when she heard him stamping his boots on the back door mat, then heard his footsteps on the stairs. Peering down through the loft hatch, unaware of the smudge of dirt across her exquisite nose, or the tangled mess of her hair, she gave a reluctant smile at his quizzical expression.

'Is this an old English pre-Christmas custom I didn't know about?' he asked sardonically, standing beneath her.

'My goodness, yes!' she said with determined friendliness. 'It's called hunt the Christmas decorations.'

'Find them?'

'Not yet.'

'Move over, then, I'll give you a hand.'

'I don't need a hand,' Sam denied hastily, not in the least liking the idea of him sharing the small loft space with her.

'Yes, you do, right on that delightful derrière. Now move over.' With a swift jump, Devlin curled his fingers over the edge of the opening, then pulled himself easily up. Settling himself beside her, he grinned.

'Cosy.'

With a little snort, she moved away from him, far more conscious than she should have been by his closeness. He smelled of outdoors, a tang of pine needles and something else, cologne perhaps, the touch of his sweater warm against her arm, his fingers cold as he touched them to her face, and she jerked away.

'What's wrong?' he asked softly, his warm breath just brushing her cheek.

'Nothing,' she denied shortly.

'Then why so touchy?'

'I'm not touchy, I just don't like the arrogant way you take control. I was perfectly capable of finding the decorations by myself!'

'Were you, now? Or can it be that the fair Selina is nervous of sharing the small, dark loft space with a man? That she's been celibate too long?' he asked suggestively.

'What the hell's that supposed to mean?'

'Only that my touch seems to disturb you for some reason.'

'Don't be ridiculous! I don't like you!'

'Oh, my poor innocent,' he taunted. 'Liking has nothing whatever to do with it.'

'It does with me,' she gritted. 'I'm not some poor deluded innocent like Julie—and even if I were, I certainly wouldn't look to you to relieve my frustration.'

'Ah, no, I was forgetting David.'

'Let's just leave David out of this, shall we?'

'Certainly. Do you have a torch?'

'Of course I have a torch!' she snapped. 'I'd hardly rummage around in the dark!'

'Wouldn't you?' he asked drily. 'Even if only to prove your superiority over us lesser mortals?' Taking the torch from her, he shone it round the loft space. 'What are they in?'

'I don't know,' she gritted, wishing she had the courage to shove him back through the loft hatch. 'But Robbie assured me this was where Julie put them after last Christmas. And I don't in the least consider myself superior to anyone else.'

'Don't you?' Devlin asked indifferently. 'Then stop trying to score points. It's difficult enough without you being on the defensive all the time.'

'I'm not...'

'Sam,' he said warningly, 'shut up.'

Lapsing into mutinous silence, squeezing herself into the smallest space possible to avoid touching him, Sam watched him play the small beam about the loft. She wasn't on the defensive—well yes, she was, but what the hell did he expect?

'Stop sulking,' he reproved mildly. 'What's that box over there?'

Tempted to tell him it was the bones of other strangers who'd had the misfortune to knock on her door, Sam bit her lip instead. 'I don't know,' she managed quietly. 'If you'll hold the torch steady, I'll crawl across and get it, I'm smaller than you.'

'And less likely to put your foot through the ceiling,' he returned drily. 'OK, be careful.'

Crawling awkwardly across the narrow beam, she reached out for the box and dragged it carefully across to him. Sitting cross-legged, determinedly shutting her mind to his disturbing presence, she investigated the contents. A carrier bag filled with books, an old scarf, a broken jug. A large brown envelope full of letters, and at the bottom a smaller box containing the decorations. Leaving the other things undisturbed, she carefully lifted out the box.

'OK, I'll go down first,' said Devlin pushing the larger box to one side. Handing her the torch, he swung himself easily down, then held up his hands to take the box of decorations.

'OK, Sam, down you come.'

'Well, I would do if you'd move out of the way,' she muttered disagreeably. Gingerly lowering her legs through the opening she waited for him to move.

'Just grab hold of the edge and lower yourself,' he instructed impatiently.

'I don't think I can.' There was something rather daunting about lowering herself into space, but it was a lot less daunting than having him catch her. 'If you put the chair back I can——'

'No, you can't—you'll end up breaking your neck. Come on, Sam, just do it!'

With a little tut, she turned and lowered herself backwards, feeling her wretched jumper catch on the rough edge. As he took hold of her feet, she let herself drop and they both went flying backwards, to land in a tangled heap on the small landing.

'Very good, Sam,' Devlin said drily. 'I said lower yourself, not jump! Are you hurt?'

'No,' she mumbled, feeling stupid. Pushing herself into a sitting position and shaking her hair off her face, she stared down at him where he still lay on his back beneath her legs. 'Sorry. Are you?'

'No.' With a smile, that she didn't think she liked very much, he levered himself up, hands flat out behind him, which brought his face a great deal too close for comfort.

'Don't,' she said automatically.

'Don't what?' he asked softly.

'Don't whatever it is you're about to do,' she warned, glaring at him.

'Get up?' he taunted. 'You want me to sit on the landing for the rest of the day?'

'Don't play games, Devlin—you know very well what I mean.'

'Mm, you mean don't do this...' and before she could stop him, he kissed her hard on the mouth, then grinned, his yellow eyes gleaming with unholy amusement between his thick dark lashes. 'I wasn't going to,' he denied outrageously. With another grin, he got lithely to his feet and extended a hand to help her up.

Ignoring it, Sam scrambled rather inelegantly to her own feet. Feeling thoroughly shaken, she gave him a look of haughty disdain and brushed past him, leaving him to bring the decorations. It was only a kiss, she told herself impatiently. No, not even a kiss. A mere touch of his mouth against hers, over before it had begun—and she felt as though she'd been branded. Scurrying down the stairs and into the lounge, she came to a shocked halt.

'Oh, Devlin!' she exclaimed, her confusion forgotten as she stared at the little fir tree leaning in the corner. 'It's perfect! Where did you find it?'

'Oh, just lying around,' he dismissed with a small smile. 'We'll probably get sued for theft as soon as the roads are open. Got a bucket or something we can put it in?'

'Mm, in the shed,' she said absently, her eyes still fixed widely on his face. 'Thank you,' she whispered awkwardly.

'My pleasure. We have a truce now, do we?' he asked, his head tilted questioningly on one side, his mouth tugged into a small smile.

Looking away, rather more disturbed by his smile than she wanted to admit, Sam nodded. 'Yes,' she agreed cautiously. 'I'm sorry I was rude earlier——'

'But you couldn't forgive me, for—despoiling your friend,' he finished for her. Pulling his coat back on, he went out to the shed.

It wasn't entirely that, she thought bleakly. In fact she wasn't sure it was that at all. Even had they met in different circumstances, she thought her reaction would probably have been the same. Devlin was too masculine, too overpowering... Cutting that thought off hastily, she knelt on the floor and pulled the box of decorations towards her. There wasn't very much. Some tinsel and baubles for the tree, a few streamers that looked as though they'd been made by Robbie—at nursery school, maybe. There weren't even any fairy lights. Disappointed, she sat back on her heels.

'What's up?' asked Devlin as he carried the now potted tree in and stood it in the window. Indicating the box, Sam pulled a face.

'Not exactly Oxford Street standard, are they?' he asked derisively as he prodded them with his fingers. 'Just as well I managed to get to the shop in the village, isn't it?'

'What?'

With another smile that held no trace of mockery, he disappeared back into the kitchen, to return moments later with a carrier bag. Delving into it, rather in the manner of a conjuror into a hat, he produced three packets of tinsel, fairy lights and some chocolate soldiers. 'It was all they had left, I'm afraid. David and I couldn't even find any holly—or mistletoe,' he added softly. 'But then we don't need any—do we?'

'No.'

'No,' he echoed, 'I didn't think we did.'

Looking at him sharply, Sam got the distinct feeling that his denial had a different interpretation from her own, and she felt her cheeks flame.

'For a beautiful lady, you're not very assured, are you?' he asked, coming to sit on the sofa next to where she knelt on the floor.

'No.'

'Why not, Sam?' he asked softly. 'And don't deny your beauty, because you're not a fool, you must know how lovely you are.'

Shrugging, she mumbled, 'I often wish I weren't.'

'Why?'

'I hate being stared at,' she retorted in some embarrassment.

'And you are certainly a lady well worth a stare,' he confirmed, amused. 'Go on, tell Uncle Devlin.'

Giving him a look of exasperation, Sam turned her face away and began fiddling with the decorations. 'People make assumptions—they seem to think that just because I look like I do I don't have the problems the rest of the world has. It's all right for you, they say. Why is it all right for me?' she demanded a shade crossly. 'Being beautiful brings more problems, not less! People either assume I'm dumb, or promiscuous, or conceited——'

'And you're none of those things?'

'No,' she denied faintly. She was never very comfortable talking about herself, and this man made her feel even more self-conscious than usual.

'What did you do before Julie got ill?' he asked, suddenly changing the subject.

'Mm?' Turning to stare at him blankly for a moment, she sighed. 'Trouble-shooter for a hotel chain.'

'Trouble-shooter?' he asked, his eyebrows shooting up in astonishment. 'You?'

'You don't need to sound so incredulous,' she reproved with a small smile. 'It merely means that I would go to work in one of the hotels that weren't profitable, try to find out why, and put it right if I could. Usually it was simply a matter of getting the right staff in the right job.'

'Mm,' he murmured, 'not as simple as you make it sound, I suspect. Did you enjoy it?'

'Yes, very much. Sir Charles Lore, who owns the chain, said he would take me back when I'd—er—resolved my domestic problems.'

'You didn't explain the reasons?'

'No. Just that there were some personal problems I needed to sort out.'

'And Paul? Where did he fit in?' he put in slyly. 'And don't glare at me, Sam, or deny it. It's as plain as a pikestaff that he let you down, or someone did.'

'He didn't let me down,' she mumbled. 'It was the other way round, if anything.'

'Told you to choose?' he asked, showing a perception she could have done without.

'Yes,' she sighed. 'We'd just got engaged when Julie became ill and I came down here to look after Robbie while she was in hospital. He wasn't very pleased.'

'No, I don't suppose he was,' he agreed. 'He presumably worked in London?'

'Yes. He got down most weekends to see me, and I went up to town when I could, but it wasn't always easy.'

'Didn't Julie have any other friends she could have asked?'

Shaking her head, Sam admitted, 'Not many, and certainly not any who knew Robbie as well as I did.'

'And not any who were prepared to give up their jobs and move down here.'

'She was my friend,' she said with a touch of defiance. 'We'd known each other since we were small—she'd have done the same for me. It's not so much to ask, from a friend, is it?' she asked quietly. 'Not so very much when you're dying.' Her throat blocked by the tears that still came too easily when she thought of her friend, she swallowed hard before continuing. 'I thought she'd get better. I never thought she'd die. When it became obvious that the treatment wasn't working and she asked me to take care of Robbie, how could I refuse? I was the only stable thing in his life at that moment; if I'd disappeared as well as his mother... I put off telling Paul for ages, until it could no longer be put off. At first he was stunned, then incredulous, then angry. He wasn't going to start married life with someone else's child. And I could hardly blame him for that. Could I?' she asked.

'He suggested you put him in care?'

'Yes.'

'But you wouldn't consider it?'

'Of course I considered it!' she retorted, turning an anguished face towards him. 'I'm only human—selfish as the rest! Of course I thought of it! To my shame I even made enquiries—only at the end of the day, I couldn't. I'd given Julie my word, and to have broken it, considered only my own needs—well, I didn't think I could have lived with myself. And he isn't any trouble,' she added hastily as though Devlin were about to contradict it. 'I love him dearly.'

'It's just that sometimes,' he put in softly, 'when you're alone, in the evenings, when Robbie's in bed asleep, you wonder how you're going to spend the next ten or so years without company, without love.'

'Yes,' she whispered, 'sometimes.' Then, giving him a defiant glance, she added, 'It will be better when we move back to London.'

'Do you really believe that, Sam?'

'Yes!' she said positively, because to believe anything else would be self-defeating, would depress her unbearably. 'It wouldn't have been so bad if we'd lived in the village, with other people—I just get a bit lonely sometimes,' she confessed. 'It's a big change from working, meeting people all the time, challenges, using my mind ... But I'll be all right. Truly,' she insisted, summoning up a smile. 'We'll wait until Robbie comes back to put up the decorations, shall we? He'll like that.'

'Sure. So why was he coming down yesterday? To try again?'

'Oh, for goodness' sake!' Sam exploded. 'Don't you ever give up? I don't know why he was coming down! He wrote last week and I rang him from the callbox in the village. He just said he was coming down to talk to me. All right? Satisfied now?'

'No. Did Julie know you'd broken up with Paul?'

'No. How could I tell her?'

'So that's why you said she didn't expect anyone to be here when I returned.'

'Yes, I imagine she thought I'd be well clear before you came home. That we wouldn't even meet—although what the hell she thought I was going to do about the cottage defeats me! Why even say it was mine? That she'd bought it from you? Why not admit it was rented?' Rented. Staring at him in sudden horror, her eyes wide, she said slowly, 'I haven't been paying any rent.'

'Haven't you? Tsk, tsk!'

'Devlin! This is not funny! I thought the cottage was mine, so naturally I haven't been paying any. Well, I can't pay any now,' she continued with embarrassed defiance. 'I shall have to pay you when I move back to London, when I get a proper job.'

'So you will,' he agreed smoothly.

Her mouth pursed, Sam swung her head away from him. 'Damn you,' she said under her breath, her throat tight. 'Damn Julie. Why in heaven's name couldn't she have told me the truth?'

'Who knows? Maybe she thought she'd complicated your life enough already—although it probably accounts for her command not to tell me about Robbie. It had obviously occurred to her that we might meet.'

'But if she hadn't told me not to, I wouldn't have, would I? Because I wouldn't have known!'

'Or maybe it was a roundabout way of ensuring you did tell me.' Devlin sighed. 'Who knows how a woman's mind works? I'll go and make some tea,' he added flatly. Getting to his feet, he went into the kitchen.

Had he managed to forget his starring role? Sam wondered bleakly. Or just managed to put it out of his mind until she'd brought the subject up? And why so curious about her relationship with Paul? And her job? It was almost as if—well, as if he was trying to find reasons for her to abandon Robbie. Only why would he do that? Frowning, she went over their conversation again, but could come to no conclusion. Perhaps he was just being nosy. Although thinking about Paul, she supposed she

would have to ring him as soon as she could get to
a phone. Tell him about Devlin. Why? her mind
insisted. Why do you need to tell him? It didn't
make any difference, did it?

Staring rather blindly down, she thought about
Paul, about the past. If Julie hadn't died, they'd
have been married by now. Would be living in a
suburban semi, and without her even realising it
her mouth turned down at the corners as she idly
smoothed out some of the crumpled decorations.
She'd have been putting up her own Christmas tree,
maybe, deciding what to have for their dinner...
Didn't sound very exciting, did it? Exciting? And
against her will, Paul's face was overstamped by
Devlin's. Devlin would be exciting... Shocked by
the way her thoughts were travelling, she shoved
the decorations back in the box and closed the lid
as though it would close off her thoughts. Disloyal
thoughts.

When Robbie returned, happy and excited from his
day with his friend, they put up the decorations,
and Sam made a determined effort to be cheerful.
When they'd eaten and Robbie was in his pyjamas
ready for bed, they sat in the lounge, the curtains
drawn against the cold night, the Christmas lights
winking comfortingly from the tree, the fire warm
and cosy. Devlin was lounging back in the armchair reading one of Sam's books, Robbie was lying
on the floor colouring and Sam was attempting to
knit a scarf. Very domestic, she thought with a
rather sour smile. Home, sweet home.

'Sam?' Robbie asked quietly, his chin propped
in his hands.

'Mm?'

'Is Mummy an angel?'

'An angel?' she asked, her mind totally blank for a moment, then with a small soft smile as she remembered her friend, she comforted, 'Yes, darling, I rather think she is. Why?'

'Is she hard?'

'Hard?'

'Yes. Peter's granny's an angel,' said Robbie, his dark eyes fixed on her face, 'and he said she was hard. He said all dead people were hard—and I just wondered if Mummy was.'

Oh, God. Glancing helplessly at Devlin, and finding no help from that quarter, just blank incomprehension, Sam stared back at Robbie. Surely they weren't into rigor mortis? 'Why did Peter think his granny was hard?' she temporised as she prayed for inspiration.

''Cos he went to see her, and she was hard!'

'Went to see her where?' she asked, puzzled. By no stretch of the imagination could she believe the Gunners would allow Peter to see their hard, dead granny.

'In the cemet'ry!' Robbie said impatiently. 'His granny was an angel and she was hard!' Then he glared at Devlin when he made a rather extraordinary sound in the back of his throat which he hastily turned into a cough.

Her lips twitching as she too realised what Robbie was talking about, Sam hastily straightened her face as Robbie turned back to her. 'And,' he continued defiantly, 'I wanted to know if Mummy was an angel like Peter's granny, and if she was, how did she fly?'

'Fly,' she repeated, her voice wobbling, then had to clamp down on a hysterical bubble of laughter as she pictured her dear, rather overweight friend immortalised as a stone angel frantically flapping solid wings in an effort to get off the ground. Oh, Julie, she thought helplessly, can you hear this? With a warm, gentle smile, she explained carefully, 'The angel Peter saw wasn't exactly his granny, just a sort of stone picture of what she would look like.' Searching her mind for words he would understand, she continued, 'His real granny is an angel up in heaven—and you can't see real angels.'

'Oh,' he said thoughtfully, a little frown on his face. Then, just as she was congratulating herself on getting out of that very nicely, he asked, 'Sam?'

'Yes, darling?'

'Didn't Mummy want a stone picture on her grave?'

'No,' she denied weakly, not knowing whether Julie had or she hadn't since the subject had never come up, then fabricated hastily, 'She thought you would rather remember her as she was, from—um—photo-pictures.'

'Oh,' he said again. His little face still troubled, he asked, 'Didn't she want flowers, Sam?' Then rather wistfully, 'Peter takes his granny flowers.'

'Oh, Robbie!' she cried, distressed. Getting to her feet, she knelt down beside him and gathered him into her arms. 'Of course she wants flowers— I never thought...' Hugging him tight, she promised, 'As soon as the snow clears we'll go. We'll buy a great big bunch of flowers and take them.'

'She'll like that, won't she, Sam?'

'Yes, darling.'

Snuggling into her arms, he whispered, 'Did Jesus want her very much? Peter said his granny died because Jesus wanted her.'

Pressing her face against his hair, her eyes squeezed shut to prevent her tears, Sam breathed huskily, 'Yes, I expect that's why.'

'He won't want you, Sam, will he?' he asked in a small voice.

Unable to do anything but shake her head and hold him tighter, she said thickly, 'No.'

'Promise, Sam?'

'I promise.'

'OK.' Wriggling free of her, he gave her one of his heartbreaking smiles, all right with his world again. 'Shall I go to bed now?'

Nodding, she managed, 'I'll be up in a minute to tuck you in. Don't forget your teeth.'

'No. Night, Sam. Night, Devlin.'

CHAPTER THREE

WHEN Robbie had gone, seeming quite content with her promise that she had no guarantee of keeping, Sam remained where she was, her hands clenched tight against her chest as though it might ease the pain there.

'I never thought,' she whispered painfully, her voice thick with tears. 'I thought it would be too distressing for him to go to her grave—I didn't know. It's so unfair!' she burst out. 'She was only twenty-five, one of the nicest people I ever knew. Good and kind and generous. She'd have done anything for anybody. Why is it always the nice ones?'

'I don't know, Sam,' Devlin said quietly, lifting her to her feet and holding her in a comforting embrace. 'You can only ever do the best you can with whatever life throws at you—you can't do more. If you'd taken him to see her grave and he'd been upset, you'd never have forgiven yourself. Don't blame yourself now for something you could never have envisaged—just don't go and die, hm?' he murmured with a too obvious attempt at humour, yet there was a thickness to his voice too.

Sniffing, Sam raised her head and searched in her pocket for a hanky. 'I shouldn't have promised, should I?'

'What else could you have done? We none of us know what fate has in store for us—and I wasn't much help. I thought you handled it very well,' he concluded, his voice now flat and empty.

Searching his face, she suddenly realised that she had never really taken his feelings into consideration, not properly. 'I'm sorry, Devlin,' she apologised quietly. 'It can't be very easy for you either.'

'No. I feel as though it isn't real. He doesn't seem like my son—God, I can't even say it without feeling stupid. Wrong. I look at him and tell myself he's mine, but there's no feeling of reality. He's just a child, a nice little boy, but that's all. He doesn't even look like me.'

'No.'

Turning away from her, he walked to the window. Moving one curtain aside, he stared out, his back hunched broodingly. 'We're not even certain he is mine—I mean, there's no conclusive proof. Only Julie's last words, and the time factor. It's not beyond the realms of possibility that there was someone else.'

'No, yet it's difficult to see how,' Sam mused, her eyes still rather haunted as she stared at his straight back. 'She was staying with me, I told you, and as far as I know all she ever did was walk in the park, mooch around in my flat. I didn't even know she'd arranged to lease this cottage until a few days before she moved in.' Thinking back to that day nearly six years ago, she tried to remember anything that might point to there having been another man. Only all she remembered of any significance was Julie talking to her mother on the phone, the row they had indulged in, Julie in a temper, her saying she was going to see if she could move in early—and that she was going to get rid of the damned phone so that no one, no one could get in touch with her! But there had never been any mention of a man. Had she been different? Secretive? Worn a secret smile? Sam didn't think so.

'Then maybe she met someone down here,' Devlin persisted.

'It's possible, I suppose, but I find it hard to believe she met someone straight away, then allowed them...' Yet she'd allowed Devlin, hadn't she? So why not someone else? And she'd lied about the cottage, so what else might she have lied about? Sam was beginning to wonder if she'd known her friend at all. So many things that didn't seem to add up to the person she thought she'd known. Staring at Devlin with a helpless expression, she genuinely tried to help, be completely fair, but she honestly couldn't see how there could have been anyone else. 'The Forresters, who always seem to know what's going on, had never seen her with anyone. In fact, they asked me if I knew who Robbie's father was. I'm afraid they were rather censorious towards her.'

'Yes, they would be. Any girl who got herself into trouble in their day would either have been forced to marry the man, or forced to have the child adopted. But they live over a mile away, hardly able to keep track of all that went on, I wouldn't have thought.'

'No,' Sam agreed lamely. 'Can't you remember anything about that night?' she asked almost desperately.

'No.' His voice bleak, Devlin gave a long sigh. 'It's snowing again.'

'Yes.' Her eyes troubled, she said, 'There are tests, aren't there? Genetic something or other. They'd tell us if you were—or weren't.'

'Yes. Oh, well, there's nothing we can do at the moment...'

'No, and this time last year who would have thought things would change so drastically? Robbie was a happy, noisy little boy, Julie's pots were selling well, beginning to make her name, and by February she was in hospital. By September, she was dead.'

'Yes, by September she was dead,' he repeated flatly, moving the curtain back across the window and turning to face her. Staring at her silently for long moments, he finally said, 'You might as well stay here until you're ready to go back to town. When did you say the tenant in your flat leaves?'

'The end of March. Are you sure? I have to confess it would be a great weight off my mind, but what about you? What will you do?' Because you can't stay here, she added mentally. No way could she remain in close proximity to this disturbing man for all those weeks.

'There's a job they've asked me to look at, a new type of suspension bridge in north Spain. I can go early, find somewhere to stay, make some preliminary tests.'

'Is that what you do?' she asked curiously. 'Build bridges?'

'Mm, and dams, whatever. I'm a structural engineer.'

'And that's why you were in Canada?'

'Yes,' he sighed, 'and before that in the Gulf.'

'And were you intending to live here permanently?'

'No, I came back to put it on the market. I've a house outside Hastings that my—father left to me. I thought I might do it up, live there. I don't know,' he muttered, still staring rather blankly at her. 'I'm tired of roving, never having a settled base. I have one or two other options I can take up. I've been offered a consultancy, or a desk job, but I don't know if I want it. The truth is, I'm bored. Thirty-six years old,' he said with a self-derisive twist to his mouth, 'and I'm bored. And tired,' he added. 'Dear God, but I'm tired!' Raking his thick hair back with both hands so that it stuck out comically, he stretched, then rested both hands on her shoulders. 'So, Selina Anne Martin, what would you recommend for a tired and jaded structural engineer?'

'I don't know,' she denied shakily, lowering her eyes from his, rather more aware of him than she should have been. Aware of the heavy warmth of his hands on her shoulders, of the rise and fall of his broad chest so close to her, of his stillness, and strength. 'A complete rest, I suppose. I'm hardly an expert on how to get your life together, am I?'

'No,' he said softly, almost intimately, and she swallowed drily, wanting desperately to move away—wanting desperately to stay. Startled by the unexpected thought, she stepped back.

'Can't we just leave things as they are for now?' she asked quickly. 'Get Christmas over with before making any decisions?'

When Devlin didn't immediately answer, she looked warily up, aware of the sudden tension that crackled between them, a tension she didn't know how to dispel. He was staring at her, but not seeing her, she thought. His eyes had a distant look to them as though he were seeing some other time, some other horizon.

'Devlin?' she prompted huskily. 'Did you hear me?'

'Yes,' he sighed. 'Yes, Sam, I heard.' Focusing his eyes back on her face, he gave a wry smile. 'Always put off till tomorrow all those things you don't want to do today, hm? All right, we'll leave all discussions until after Christmas. Another day isn't going to change anything, is it?'

'No.' Only things had already changed, hadn't they? And she didn't know how to change them back. She wished with all her heart he had never come to disturb their peace. 'I'd better go and tuck Robbie in,' she murmured awkwardly, and with an odd distracted smile she left him and went upstairs.

After kissing Robbie goodnight and tucking him in, she stood in her room staring from the window, delaying the moment when she must face Devlin again. Had she seriously misjudged him? He'd been different today, kinder, softer, that abrasive sarcasm missing. Was this the real Devlin Howe? Or was it that other man, the man of yesterday? Yesterday's man would be easier to cope with. When he'd been holding her, she'd had the most overwhelming desire to lean against him, slide her arms around him, be held, kissed. And that was the craziest thing of all—because she was still in love with Paul. Yet she couldn't even conjure up his face. Only Devlin's, and the traitorous thought intruded that Paul would not have been gentle with her, compassionate after Robbie's outburst. He would simply have told her to pull herself together. Perhaps she and Paul had lived too closely in each other's pockets to be able to see each other clearly.

He had obviously considered she would find it no problem to put Robbie in a home, and she had thought Paul would have understood her need to look after her friend's child. They'd seen each other every evening, gone to the theatre, films, had a drink, and then stayed in while they saved to be married, yet they'd never talked. Not really talked about themselves, their hopes, their dreams. Oh, they'd talked about their jobs, what sort of house they'd like, but not shared their inner selves. She'd had more intimate conversations with Devlin than she'd ever had with Paul.

Feeling troubled and confused, she went back to the lounge.

They spent the evening quietly, not saying much, both thinking their own thoughts, yet Sam was terribly conscious of Devlin's presence. Raising her eyes slightly so that she could watch him through her lashes, she examined that strong, tanned face, the untidy brown hair with those ridiculous streaks. His lashes were long and thick, she saw as he stared down at the book on his lap. His hands were strong, the nails clean and short, the pads of his fingers callused, not soft like Paul's. A man's hands, capable. What would it be like to have those hands touch her——? With a little snatched breath, she broke the thought midway, because thoughts of being held by him, touched by him, were too dangerous for words.

Leaning back in the chair, she transferred her gaze to the Christmas tree, stared blindly, until the lights blurred and danced before her eyes. The ticking of the clock seemed over-loud in the small room, seemed to magnify their aloneness. She heard Devlin shift slightly in his chair and knew he was watching her, could feel his eyes on her, and her nerves tightened, stretched, until with a little husky cry, she said, 'Don't.'

'Don't what, Sam?' he asked softly.

'Watch me,' she whispered, embarrassed.

'But you're a lady well worth watching. I make you nervous, don't I?'

'Yes,' she said crisply, her voice too loud in the still room. Pushing the wretched knitting down the side of the chair, she got abruptly to her feet. 'I'm going to bed,' she announced somewhat defiantly. She wouldn't sleep, she knew that, but she couldn't stay here a moment longer feeling trapped—and guilty.

'You won't sleep,' he purred.

'I know!' she shouted, whirling round on him, her sudden burst of temper out of all proportion to his comment. She knew she wouldn't sleep, dammit! 'But I can't—I'm not used——'

'To company? To a man sitting in your lounge?' Devlin finished for her. 'Relax, Sam, nothing will happen that you don't want to happen.'

'I don't want anything to happen,' she denied. Yet even to her own ears her voice didn't sound convincing. He looked so—so bland, sitting there, so amused by her discomfort, and she glared at him, her green eyes too bright, her face clearly reflecting her warring emotions. So much had happened in such a short space of time, too much, and he was like no man she had ever met—unpredictable, his moods swinging oddly from one to another, leaving her bewildered and unsure of herself. The pool of light from the table lamp spilled across his hair, turning it to gold, left his face in shadow, making him a stranger. Yet in essence, that was what he was, a stranger. She knew very little about him, about his life.

'I've made up the camp-bed up in Robbie's room. It's not very big, but I thought it would be better than the sofa. Or you could have my bed,' she added, striving to remain calm when he didn't answer.

'With you in it?' he taunted.

'No!' she exclaimed, horrified. 'Of course not with me in it! Oh,' she muttered crossly when he grinned, 'I'm going to bed.'

Yet once in her room, she made no attempt to undress or wash, just stood at the window shivering, her arms hugged round herself, staring at the gently drifting snowflakes. Was that what he'd said to Julie? 'With you in it?' And she'd said yes? The thought was somehow painful, and she wrenched her mind away.

Christmas, she thought, desperately trying to divert her worrying thoughts. It would be Christmas Eve tomorrow. Last year she had spent Christmas and New Year with her parents on Madeira where they now lived. Dad had taken early retirement and they'd bought a villa out there. Where would she be next year? And where had Devlin intended to spend Christmas? Here on his own? With friends?

Sam stood there for a long time allowing her thoughts to drift until she became conscious of how cold she was. Grabbing her nightdress she hurried along to the bathroom.

When she woke in the morning, the snow had stopped, the sky was a bright, clear blue. Which it shouldn't have been, she suddenly realised. Not at eight in the morning. Turning on her side, she peered at her bedside clock—and saw to her horror that it was nearly ten o'clock. Heavens, why had no one woken her? About to scramble hastily out of bed, she paused as she heard Robbie squeal with laughter. Grabbing her robe, she went to the window. A magnificent snowman stood proudly in the middle of the back garden, and Robbie and Devlin were noisily pelting it with snowballs. Her face softening, Sam watched them for a few moments. It looked like fun—and fun had been something missing from both their lives for such a long time, and she felt a pang of guilt. It had been so difficult to know the best way to deal with Robbie. It had seemed wrong somehow to go on trips to the zoo, the seaside—not that the weather had been ideal for that, but days out. Had she been handling it all wrong? Had her own grief and insecurity overshadowed the child's needs? Devlin had known him a few short hours, yet he seemed to understand Robbie without effort. Without the mental gymnastics she went through.

A bright fire was burning in the grate when she went down, porridge bubbling on the stove, tea in the pot. Nursing a cup of tea, she watched them through the kitchen window. She'd have liked to have joined them, but felt her presence might be an intrusion, which was ridiculous. Devlin was the intruder, yet it was she who was robbed of confidence. She hadn't been like that before he came, had she? As he caught sight of her, Robbie aimed a snowball at her, and more by luck than judgement it spattered against the window. Shaking a fist at him, Sam grinned. He looked happy, like a normal five-year-old, his cheeks rosy from his exertions, his eyes bright. Devlin too looked more relaxed, as though he was enjoying himself. His brown hair was ruffled by the wind, his strong legs planted apart as he formed another snowball, his eyes on her through the window.

'Coming out?' he mouthed, and Sam shook her head.

'Coward!' Smiling, she turned away to wash up. They would look to any passer-by like a normal, happy family. Only they weren't. They were two strangers brought together by fate. A malicious fate?

After lunch of egg and chips, they all went out to clear the path, for what reason, Sam wasn't sure. They couldn't go anywhere until the snow-ploughs came through. Still, it tired Robbie out, and that was to the good. Christmas Eve was not a time for getting children to sleep easily. He'd had his stocking ready to hang up since three o'clock, and by six, Sam was getting a little tired of his constant demands to know the time. A glass of sherry and a mince pie were on the little table in the lounge ready for Father Christmas, and she had reassured the anxious child for at least the fifth time that yes, Father Christmas would be able to get down the chimney, and no, she wouldn't forget to put the fire out before he came.

'Bed, Robbie,' Devlin put in quietly, his voice firm.

With a rather calculating look that Sam had never seen on his face before, Robbie turned to face Devlin. 'I don't have to,' he said defiantly. 'Sam doesn't make me go to bed if I don't want to.'

'I'm not Sam, and when I say bed, young man, I mean bed. It's not a subject for discussion, for argument. Now go!'

'Sam——'

'Bed!' roared Devlin and Robbie scampered away, his face mutinous. Devlin smiled. Turning to Sam, he said easily, 'That young gentleman is getting spoiled.'

'Nonsense, he's just over-excited, that's all,' she returned stiffly, not in the least amused that Devlin was able to handle Robbie much better than she had done. 'And even if he is, he needs a little spoiling after all he's been through. Even you can't expect him to adjust overnight!'

'Oh, we're back to even me, are we?' he asked softly, a rather dangerous glint in his eyes. 'And it's three months since his mother died, not exactly overnight!'

'Three months isn't so very long. Anyway, it's Christmas, and all children should be spoiled——'

'I know it's Christmas,' he said with exaggerated patience. 'That doesn't mean he has to be rude. He's over-tired, excited, and he needs a firm hand.'

'Yes, mine!' she exclaimed, refusing to back down, even though she knew he was right, but he'd been correcting Robbie all day, overruling her, and she felt resentful and hurt that a comparative stranger was able to handle the boy better than she. 'It might be your cottage, Devlin, and we might be here on sufferance, but that doesn't give you the right to ride roughshod over everyone.'

'Telling him to go to bed isn't riding roughshod, and why so argumentative all of a sudden?'

'I'm not being argumentative,' she denied irritably. 'Merely pointing out that it's none of your business!' Then she swung round, startled, as someone banged heavily on the back door.

'Probably lover boy come to give you your Christmas kiss,' Devlin sneered sourly.

'Don't be ridiculous! And we'll leave David out of this, if you don't mind!' Stomping angrily into the kitchen, Sam yanked open the back door. 'Hello, David,' she said peremptorily. 'Coming in?'

'Oh, dear!' he exclaimed comically. 'Chose a bad time, did I?'

'No, it's all right,' she said stiltedly, 'just Robbie playing up. Sorry, I didn't mean to bite your head off. Would you like a cup of tea or something?'

'No, can't stay. I only really came out to take Brandy for a walk; I told Barbs I wouldn't be long.' Moving one hand from behind his back, David thrust a carrier bag awkwardly at her, and lowering his voice whispered, 'Just a few things for under the tree. I didn't know what to get Devlin,' he murmured, lowering his voice still further, his face close to Sam's, 'so I wrapped a bottle of Scotch. Will that be all right, do you think?'

'Oh, David, there was no need, but thank you.' And because she liked him, because he was kind and she was feeling unwanted and thoroughly unloved, she pressed a warm kiss on his mouth. 'Happy Christmas, David, and thank you.'

With a wide grin, and a laugh, he caught her up in a bear-hug and kissed her back. 'I do so love Christmas!' he exclaimed exuberantly. 'All this kissing and cuddling with pretty girls is so good for my ego!' With another quick hug, he turned and left, and Sam walked slowly back to the lounge, a soft smile on her mouth. A smile that shrivelled and died as she caught Devlin's derisory look. Tilting her chin defiantly, she put the presents David had brought beneath the tree.

'Just can't stay away, can he?'

'Obviously not!' she snapped.

'And it doesn't bother you that he's married?'

'No, why should it?'

'Why indeed?' he queried, his voice flat and hard. 'Any port in a storm, eh, Sam?'

'Oh, just hark at the pot calling the kettle black,' she sneered sarcastically. 'It's all right for you to do as you please, but let anyone else do it, and it's moral rectitude time. David is just a friend, as I've told you before, and why you have to keep hurling him in my teeth, I can't imagine.'

'Presumably for the same reason you keep hurling Julie in mine.'

'I do not keep hurling her!' she gritted. 'I've barely mentioned her!'

'You don't need to; every time you look at me it's written clear on your face. The Great Seducer!'

'If the cap fits...'

'But it doesn't,' he denied as he caught her arms in a brutal grip and held her in front of him, 'and even if it were true, there's a great deal of difference between that situation and this. Julie wasn't married.'

'No, just innocent—and a moment's snatched pleasure on your part does not give you the right to interfere in our lives! You were kind enough to let us stay over Christmas, and I'm grateful,' said Sam in a voice that made it perfectly clear she wasn't grateful at all, 'but I do not need your help in organising my private life, nor in chastising Robbie!'

'No, it's much more gratifying to play sole martyr, isn't it, Sam?' Devlin derided, by now as angry as she.

'That's a lousy thing to say! I love Robbie! I couldn't have loved him more if he'd been my own son!'

'And that's it, isn't it, Sam? He's not your son, but you persist in playing out the fantasy that he is! Paul wouldn't play, so you've transferred your yearnings to David! You're twenty-five, not a teenager! So stop playing bloody house and use some common sense for once! That child needs discipline too, not just someone who will indulge his every whim!'

'I do not indulge his every whim!' she shouted. 'And may I remind you that it was I who gave up my job, my flat, my friends, to look after him? It was I who held Julie's hand when she was dying! I who coped these last months! Not you, who didn't give a twopenny damn about anyone but yourself, swanning around the world playing with bridges! You didn't have to sit up with him every night while he cried himself to sleep! You didn't have to beg the bank manager to give you an overdraft just so that you could afford to eat! Me—not you! And that gives me the right to bring him up as I think fit! I may not be doing it perfectly, but I'm doing my best!'

'I didn't say you weren't!'

'Just that my best wasn't good enough!'

'Stop putting words in my mouth!' Devlin retorted furiously. 'I was trying to help! The boy needs discipline!'

'He gets discipline!' she gritted.

'When?'

'When I think he needs it!' she yelled incensed. Dragging herself from his grip, she pushed him to one side. 'I'm going up to tuck him in!'

'I will go and tuck him in,' he contradicted savagely. 'And perhaps while I'm gone you'll give some serious thought to your behaviour. Trading insults with me is not the way to promote your case! Neither is playing footsy with David at every conceivable opportunity! I may not have any rights,' he continued inexorably, his voice as bleak and unforgiving as the snowy landscape, 'but what sort of man would it make me if I ignored the whole thing? Opted out? So stop cutting off your nose to spite your face. You need help; don't be too proud to accept it.'

'And what happens when you're no longer around?' Sam asked bitterly.

'By then you will maybe have learned a much needed lesson. And if you so desperately need a man, use me, don't wreck someone else's marriage just because you're frustrated!' Releasing her, he stalked out and upstairs.

'And for that I'm supposed to be grateful?' she choked. 'The great Devlin Howe will show us how it's done? Well, let me tell you,' she ran out to shout after him, 'I wouldn't touch Julie's cast-offs with a ninety-foot pole!'

Rushing back into the lounge, she slammed the door. Her chest heaving, her hands clenched angrily at her sides, she stormed up and down the small room, her eyes too bright, her face flushed. How dared he? she raged. How bloody dared he? Playing house? Playing out a fantasy? She'd been worrying sick, anguishing over everything she did! Was she doing her best for him? Comforting him? Giving him the right things to eat? Hurling herself on to the sofa, she grabbed the cushion and hugged it to her as she stared blindly into the fire.

All right, so Robbie did need discipline, she knew he did, but how could she be firm with him when he looked so woebegone? When he still so desperately missed his mother? It was all right for Devlin Howe; he didn't love the boy! He hadn't loved Julie! As her temper abated, Sam gazed miserably into the flames, feeling inadequate and lost. And why had he got into such a temper about everything? For someone who, by his own admission, never got involved in other people's troubles, he'd surely gone to town this time. And what the hell difference did it make to him if she was involved with David? And she didn't in the least understand what he'd meant about him hurling David in her teeth for the same reason she hurled Julie. All right, so maybe she did find it hard to forget, or forgive that Devlin had made love to her friend, but only because she'd loved Julie. He didn't love anybody, so why on earth should it matter to him?

It was a long time before Devlin returned, and he came in very quietly and stood by the fire, leaning one shoulder against the mantel, his hands thrust into his pockets. Eyeing him resentfully, Sam decided she would ignore him. He could do as he damned well pleased; if he wanted to talk, all he would get in reply would be a dignified silence.

'I wasn't playing house,' she informed him stonily, overriding her resolution because she found she couldn't stand the long, oppressive silence that followed. 'And I was not acting out a fantasy.'

'No, I know. I was angry, and when I'm angry I say a lot of things I don't mean. No need to brood on it, I'll be gone soon.'

'Yes,' she agreed flatly, and the knowledge brought no comfort at all. 'Is he asleep?' she asked haughtily.

'Yes.'

'Did you speak to him?'

'Yes, Sam, I spoke to him,' he agreed wearily.

Not knowing what else to say, Sam lapsed into silence until the tension in the small room became too much to bear. As she was about to leap to her feet, to go anywhere, somewhere, Devlin suddenly spoke, and she slumped back down again.

'What did you get him for Christmas?'

'Two of those big trucks with the wide wheels,' she told him stiffly, 'one with a gravel hopper, one for carrying bricks, wood, whatever. Some Lego, one of those transformer things that start off as a robot and turn into a car.' She gave a faint, sad smile. She'd been more fascinated with its workings than a child would have been. 'Bits and pieces for his stocking, books...' which had put her bank account even further in the red.

'And what happens when he's older?' asked Devlin quietly. 'Wants a bike, a computer—how will you afford those? What happens when he wants to know who his father is?'

'I don't know. I never said I was perfect, Devlin. I'll worry about that when it comes.' Stiffening defensively, expecting another lecture, Sam glared at him balefully. Did he really think her so insensitive that she hadn't already considered all he'd said? They were thoughts that were already ever-present in her mind. Once Robbie went to school, mixed with other boys, wouldn't he begin to question his different existence? Unable to take any more, she got quickly to her feet. 'I'll go and make some coffee.'

'And play ostrich?'

'I'm not playing ostrich!' she denied wearily. 'What the hell am I supposed to do? Fabricate some story about his father dying or something? Or were you intending to put yourself forward without knowing for sure if you are? I already told you I'd handle each problem as it comes!' Walking out to the kitchen, she filled the kettle and slammed it on the Aga. What was he trying to do? Prove her unfit to take care of Robbie? Didn't he know she had enough doubts about her ability without him making them worse? And if he was Robbie's father? What then? Would he want to take him away? Closing her eyes, she leaned her forehead tiredly against the cold wall. Dear God, he couldn't do that, could he?

'Just because I didn't know of his birth, it doesn't lessen the responsibility,' Devlin said quietly from behind her, making her jump and straighten defensively. 'Even if I can't feel anything for him, I can at least help financially.'

'I don't need you to help financially,' she denied exhaustedly. 'I told you I can manage.'

'Can you? Pride won't pay the bills, Sam. And I don't know why you're so reluctant to accept help. I should have thought you'd have been grate-ful——'

'Well, I'm not,' Sam muttered awkwardly.

With a sound of exasperation, he caught her arm and turned her to face him. 'You talk about not being able to live with yourself if you'd put him in a home—do you think I'd find it easy to live with myself if my son lacked the things other children take for granted? It might only be money, but it'd be a pretty lean world without it. When we were in the garden, I asked him what he wanted from Father Christmas. He said he didn't know. He'd have liked a bike, he said, but he didn't think he'd get one because Peter said you had to have a daddy to ask for big things like that. How the hell do you think that made me feel, Sam?'

Searching his eyes, seeing only concern there, Sam lowered her lashes. Hurt for him, hurt for Robbie, hurt for herself, she whispered huskily. 'He never said—and I wish Peter wouldn't take it upon himself to become Robbie's mentor!' she added with a crotchety little twitch. 'It was never Julie's intention that he should be a burden—just——'

'Just a need to die in peace.'

'Yes.'

'Sure in the knowledge that her friend would cope.' Sighing deeply, Devlin turned away and began ranging moodily round the tiny kitchen, touching pots, picking them up, putting them down, unsettling her further.

'You expect me to walk away, Sam? Forget about him? Is that it?'

'No—I don't know. How can I know?' she exclaimed helplessly. 'I haven't had time to think. You came as such a shock. It never occurred to me I'd ever meet you. I don't even know what I expected...'

'Pipe and slippers man?' he asked rather sardonically, coming to a halt in front of her.

'Maybe. I only know I didn't expect someone so...' Searching for a word to describe him, she shrugged. Virile? Rugged? Disturbingly attractive? She didn't really know if she'd had a mental image of Devlin—all she did know with any certainty was that his appearance had given her one hell of a shock. And was continuing to do so. Was turning her whole world upside-down.

'And I didn't expect to be confronted by an astonishingly beautiful woman who was as nervous and agitated as a cat, yet in her beautiful green eyes a hurt bewilderment that intrigued me. A generous mouth that was made for a man's kisses.'

'No,' she denied almost inaudibly, wanting to move, shove him away, run, deny the sudden feeling of excitement and warmth inside her, because it was shaming, because it was almost an admission of his earlier taunts about her being frustrated.

'Yes, Sam,' he contradicted gently, his hands once more a warm, heavy weight on her shoulders, his eyes intent on her exquisite face. 'At the best of times I'm a cynic, at the worst, an arrogant bastard who goes his own way regardless. Only one man ever had my trust, my love, if you like: Nathan Howe. He gave me his name, gave me an identity— he gave me time. Time to grow, to learn, and when I'd learned, fought my way upwards in the big bad world, he died. Died before I could repay him, prove his trust in me hadn't been misplaced. I'd been to his funeral the day Julie came...'

'Which was why you were drinking,' she whispered, her eyes fixed on his throat.

'Yes.'

'You were an orphan? Nathan Howe adopted you?' she asked, moving her eyes slowly up to his, and when he nodded, she asked, puzzled, 'Then surely you of all people should understand why I didn't want Robbie to go into a home.'

'I do—but don't you see how guilty that makes me feel? He's not your responsibility, he's mine—or it looks very much as though he is—and I don't want it,' Devlin finished quietly, his eyes empty, blank, filled with guilt. 'I'm a loner, Sam, I don't need people. Don't wish to consider their needs, don't want their problems dumped on me...'

'Then don't let them,' she said earnestly, her eyes fixed entreatingly on his face. 'I know you think I'm unfit to look after him——'

'Oh, Sam, I didn't say that.'

'Yes, you did, or implied it, but don't you see? Robbie needs constancy. We don't know for sure that you're his father, and supposing, just supposing it turns out you're not? How's he going to feel when you disappear from his life? He will have been disrupted needlessly.'

'And if it turns out I am his father, Sam?'

'I don't know,' she admitted helplessly. 'But you said yourself you didn't want problems dumped on you...'

'I don't, didn't—yet there's a small boy who was conceived in a blurred memory, and although part of me wants to walk away, wash my hands of it, there's also curiosity to want to know how he'll be at eight, fifteen. Will he be like me? Will he have my temper?'

'Then why can't we just keep in touch?' she asked eagerly, seeing a solution to all their problems. 'I can write, send you photographs—and maybe when he's older he could come to you for holidays...'

'And you think that will satisfy him? Ultimately?'

'I don't know,' she wailed. 'How can either of us know? As you said before, we can only do our best. Can't we take each day as it comes? Enjoy tomorrow, for Robbie's sake? Please?'

'You make it very difficult for me to refuse when you ask like that,' he reproved, his eyes suddenly darkening. Lowering his lashes for a moment, he took a deep breath. 'All right, Sam,' he agreed quietly, 'we'll leave it for now.' Reaching past her, he took the boiling kettle off the stove. 'I'll make the coffee—have you finished wrapping his presents?'

'Yes,' she confirmed, grateful for the reprieve.

'Got any wrapping paper left?'

'A bit,' she said, surprised. 'Did you need some?'

'Yes, Sam,' he murmured, a faint twitch to his mouth. 'I managed to get some things in the local shop.' Then with a little shrug of embarrassment, he admitted, 'I bought him a train set. Not a very good one, they were limited for choice, but...'

With a warm smile, the first genuine smile she had given him, liking him suddenly, instead of just reacting to him, because embarrassment and uncertainty were such very human qualities, Sam teased, 'So that you could play with it? That's why most men buy them, isn't it?'

'Is it?' he asked wryly. 'I don't know. I told myself it was something Robbie would really like—but yes, I suspect it was entirely selfish.' Giving her a little push, he took two mugs out of the cupboard, and Sam walked thoughtfully back to the lounge.

She had thought Devlin hard, uncaring—oh, exciting, overpowering, arrogant, but she hadn't allowed him to have frailties. She'd created a black and white image—and she'd been wrong. Did he hide his real self very carefully away? So that no one would know of the soft core inside? Without fully being aware of it, she had accepted him, she thought slowly. She even actually quite liked having him here—and she was then startled by the admission. But it was true, she enjoyed his company, when he wasn't being provocative, that was. Or did she enjoy that too? The feeling, if she was honest, of flirting with danger? She'd insisted to herself that she didn't because she'd felt it wrong, because of Paul, because he'd seduced Julie. Yet liking for Devlin had grown without her realising it. And if he was Robbie's father? And she sent him away? Would Robbie one day resent her for depriving him of his father? But how could he stay? Even if he wanted to?

CHAPTER FOUR

WHEN Devlin came in, he perched on the arm of the settee where Sam was sitting and handed her a mug. '"Twas the night before Christmas,"' he quoted softly, '"when all through the house Not a creature was stirring, not even a mouse."' With a small smile, he confessed, 'I don't remember the rest.'

'No. Something about children hanging their stockings by the chimney with care, in the hope that St Nicholas soon would be there. My mother always remembered it all the way through, I expect I had a book somewhere when I was small.'

'Do you have any brothers and sisters, Sam?'

'No. Only me—I don't think my mother could have any more children.' Turning to look up at him, she examined his face. It seemed curiously bleak, and yet yearning, and she felt unexpectedly guilty. 'I'm sorry,' she apologised softly, 'were you remembering your own childhood? Was it very wretched, Devlin?'

'Wretched? No, I don't think it was wretched— a bit sterile, maybe. I was never one for yearning after the might-have-beens, even when I was small.' Giving her a penetrating look, he said quietly, 'Don't make honour and duty a shrine at which you worship, will you, Sam? Don't make him feel beholden? I know you don't want to discuss it now, but will you promise me that if it becomes too much you'll write? I suddenly find I don't want him to be—oh, hell, I don't know what I do want.' With a long sigh that tugged at her heart, Devlin put his mug in the fireplace. 'I'm going for a walk, Sam, get some fresh air.'

About to point out the pitfalls of doing anything so silly, about it being cold, snowy, Sam closed her mouth with a snap and merely nodded instead. He was old enough to know his own mind, do as he wished, and he sounded as muddled as she felt. She supposed he had his own guilt to contend with, much as he didn't want to admit it. Someone else with chickens that came home to roost unexpectedly.

She thought it might be wise to go up to her room before he came back, avoid any of the awkward silences of the night before—or the eruption of both their tempers, caused by tension, and proximity, at least on her part—although she couldn't go to bed, she had Robbie's stocking to fill, and reindeer tracks to make, she thought with a smile. Her father had done that when she was a child, made sledge and reindeer tracks on the roof one year when they had actually had snow. She could still remember the thrill and excitement she had felt when she first saw them. Looking after a child wasn't always a task; there was fun too. And you're just a great big kid, she taunted herself—but she still smiled. And she did love him; it wasn't a fantasy, as Devlin had accused. She might yearn to go back to work, but she couldn't envisage a future without Robbie. There was a curiosity in her too to see how he would turn out at fifteen, twenty-one. Oh, Julie, she thought with a sigh, why couldn't you have told me about Devlin?

Tiptoeing along the landing, she removed the
stocking from the end of Robbie's bed and took it
into her room ready for filling. Taking down the
suitcase from the top of her wardrobe, she extracted
Robbie's presents, and only then realised that she
didn't have anything for Devlin. Plumping down
on the edge of the bed, she frowned in thought.
What could she give him? She didn't have anything
suitable for a man—yes, she did, she suddenly remembered. She had bought her father the new
Wilbur Smith book, but she hadn't posted it to him
because it would have been too expensive. She'd
been going to take it when next she went out.
Getting to her feet, she ran lightly down to collect
a piece of wrapping paper, then nipped back before
Devlin returned. She would put it under the tree
when Devlin had gone to bed.

Huddled up under the quilt, still fully dressed, Sam
waited a good half an hour after she heard Devlin
go to bed before she crept downstairs. With a little
grin, she tied the cake icing nozzle on the end of
the broom—with luck, to a five-year-old they would
look like hoofprints. She could use the end of the
broom to make the sledge tracks. Pulling on her
coat, she carefully unlocked the back door. Devlin's
footprints were the only ones visible, and she
grinned again. If she trod where he had there would
be only one set of tracks—Father Christmas's. So
long as it didn't snow in the night, she thought rue-
fully. Glancing up, she saw that the sky was clear,
bright, filled with stars. So far, so good. All it
needed now, of course, was for Robbie to wake up,
come into her room and look out and ask what the
devil she was doing. Except it wasn't Robbie, it was

Devlin, and Sam jumped nearly a foot in the air as he called softly to her from the open back door.

'Is this another Christmas custom I don't know about, Sam?'

'Shh!' she warned urgently, nearly falling over in her haste to turn and shut him up. 'And don't come out, you'll ruin the footprints!'

She distinctly saw him shake his head at her before she turned back to her task. He probably thought she was nuts, and so she probably was, but she was thoroughly enjoying herself, she found. When she had finished her artistic efforts to her complete satisfaction, she trod carefully back to the cottage. Handing the broom to a grinning Devlin, dressed as he had been earlier in a thick sweater and jeans, she walked quietly in and closed the door with a soft click.

'Father Christmas has just been,' she whispered. 'You can have the sherry and the mince pie.'

'Gee, thanks. Here, I made you a hot drink.' Pushing her down to sit at the table, Devlin handed her a hot mug, then bent to remove her snow-caked slippers.

'Couldn't you have put your boots on, Sam? Your feet are soaking!'

'I didn't want to blur your footsteps,' she explained, giving a little shiver as his warm hands removed her socks and began to rub her cold feet.

'Better?' he asked softly.

'Mm,' she mumbled, her face buried in her mug. And it was—too nice. The feel of his palms on her feet was stirring all sorts of riotous feelings inside her. Dangerous feelings, warm, woolly, wanting feelings, and she took a deep ragged breath in an effort to dismiss them. Or at least bury them. His forehead was brushing her knees as he knelt before her; she'd only have to stretch her fingers out the tiniest fraction to be able to touch his hair, run her fingers through it, curve her palm to the nape of his neck. Ah, don't Sam, don't! As Devlin suddenly looked up, caught her staring, she flushed and looked hastily away, her heart jerking unevenly in her chest.

'What is it, Sam?' he asked gently.

'Nothing,' she muttered.

'Nothing,' he echoed. Getting to his feet, he took her mug away and placed it on the table before pulling her unresistingly to her feet. 'Look at me, Sam.'

'No,' she mumbled, her head down, her hair falling to obscure her face. Not that her denial made any difference; it didn't. Devlin merely put a finger beneath her chin and tilted it upward.

'Don't be afraid of feelings, Sam. Just because I'm a stranger, it doesn't mean you shouldn't have them. Everyone needs to be held, loved. Sometimes it seems the most important thing in the whole world—comfort, reassurance, closeness.' Folding her gently in his arms, he rested his head on top of hers. 'You've been buried alive in this God-forsaken place with only a small boy for company for nigh on three months. Do you think it's so terrible to want human contact?'

Lifting her head, she stared into his face. 'But you said—about David—about...'

'I was angry,' he admitted simply. 'And I didn't want you to be the sort of woman who would break up a happy marriage...'

'I'm not.'

'No,' he murmured gently, rubbing one thumb across her lower lip until it tingled. 'But we all need someone, some time.'

'Even you?' she whispered, unconsciously wriggling closer to his strong body, sliding her arms round his waist so that she could hold him.

'Even me.'

With a little sigh of pleasure, Sam admitted that yes, this was what she had wanted—to be held, just for a moment, to feel safe, needed. 'Thank you,' she said softly. 'I just needed a hug, a little cuddle.' Then she gave a soft laugh that made him lift his head and tilt hers up so that he could see her face. 'I sound like a little girl, don't I?'

'A very lovely little girl,' Devlin approved. 'A very lovely and warm little girl. Merry Christmas, Sam,' he said huskily.

Watching almost mesmerised as his face lowered, grew blurred, Sam groaned and lifted her mouth to touch his. Warmth and softness and a beautiful feeling of pleasure in her tummy, her groin. With a little mumbled sound of satisfaction she slid her arms to his neck, slipped her fingers into his thick hair and relaxed fully against him. His palms were warm on her back, soothing her, moving from her shoulder-blades to her hips and back again, and she stretched, fitting her body to his, moulding herself to his masculine curves as the kiss deepened, as his mouth parted hers, his warm breath filled her mouth. It was beautiful, something special, an exchange, a promise almost, and when he broke the kiss, reluctantly it seemed, she gave a long sigh of pleasure and opened her eyes.

'That was nice,' she breathed, her face gentle, beautiful, her extraordinary eyes almost luminous.

'Yes, it was,' he agreed softly, his expression unexpectedly tender as he gazed down at her. 'Not frightened of me any more?'

'I don't know that it was a case of being frightened,' she denied with a soft smile. 'More a case of confusion. You made me question things I didn't want to question, so I lashed out. I misjudged you, I'm sorry.'

'Understandable. An angry stranger barrelling in—and I've hardly gone out of my way to make you think any better of me since.' Holding her loosely, his eyes still on her face, Devlin continued quietly, 'Although I doubt you could think any worse of me than I do of myself.'

'No,' she denied gently, 'I don't think badly of you. You put me on the defensive, made me lose my temper. I've never met anyone like you, so sure of himself.' Then she smiled and placed a hand over his mouth as he tried to argue. 'Appearing very sure of himself,' she corrected. 'I found it hard to come to terms with the thought of you and Julie... And I didn't know why it should matter so much. I had no right to judge either of you.'

'Who had more right?' he asked quietly, his expression sombre. 'You're the one who had to bear the brunt of our behaviour. Dear God, I still can't take it in—and I certainly didn't intend to take advantage of you. You looked so little and cold,' he smiled, 'and good old Devlin wanted to comfort.'

'I wanted comfort too, a selfish desire to be held, wanted...'

'Not selfish, Sam.' With a wry smile, he continued, 'We've both been under a lot of pressure, forced into proximity. And you're a very beautiful lady—and I'm only human.'

'Like me,' she responded, touching her mouth very gently to his before laying her head against him. She felt his lips touch her temple, without urgency, without demand, his arms draw her closer, and they held each other gently, a need perhaps in them both for an interlude of peace. With a contented sigh, she moved her head and nestled it into his neck, her lips touching his warm skin, her fingers tracing his scalp so that he shivered.

'You taste nice,' she said huskily, enjoying the feel of him, the strength.

'So do you, Sam. So do you.'

Raising her head, she gave him a grateful smile. 'Thank you, I feel better now. I'd best go to bed, hadn't I?'

'Yes, Sam, best go to bed.' Putting her away from him, Devlin gave her a crooked smile. 'You go and deal with the stocking, I'll dispose of the sherry and mince pie.'

Nodding, she slipped past him and upstairs. Standing at her window, her arms hugged round herself for warmth, she stared down at the faint outline of her handiwork on the lawn, a small smile on her lips. Devlin would be someone very easy to love, the thought slipped into her mind. It wouldn't have to be worked at, like Paul. All those months of resenting him, needing him, and now, she thought, she no longer cared. So fickle, Sam? So easily diverted? Like Julie? She thought she no longer knew anything about anything.

Devlin woke her with a cup of tea at seven-thirty the next morning. He was already dressed in a thick wool shirt and grey trousers. Seeing her glance, he gave a self-mocking grin. 'I dressed up for Christmas.'

'You look very nice,' Sam told him a trifle shyly as she remembered their odd behaviour of the night before. Remembered how she'd gone to bed feeling warm and comforted—and liking him very much. She'd gone to sleep with a silly smile on her face and she had a horrible feeling it was still there.

'Thank you,' he accepted drily. 'So do you.'

Feeling a wave of pink wash into her cheeks, she hastily dragged the duvet up to cover herself.

'I left you to sleep as long as I could,' he continued, his eyes reflecting his amusement, 'but Robbie is now becoming impatient to show you his presents.'

'What time did he wake you?' she asked as she hauled herself upright. She must look a sight; why couldn't he have knocked first?

'Five,' he said wryly.

'I'm sorry. I didn't hear a thing.'

'Why apologise? I imagine he wakes you early most mornings. Make the most of a lie-in while you can. And, speaking of presents, Happy Christmas, Sam.' Moving one hand out from behind his back, Devlin presented her with a large wrapped parcel, then, perching on the edge of the bed and bending forward, kissed her lightly on the mouth. When she only continued to stare at him in confusion, he grinned. Taking her tea out of her hand and putting it on the side table, he laid the present on her knees so that he had both hands free, and before she could register his intent he pulled her gently into his arms and kissed her properly, his mouth warm and soft— and a wave of excitement and pleasure shot through her. 'Happy Christmas—again,' he whispered against her mouth before sitting back with what sounded remarkably like a reluctant sigh.

'Happy Christmas,' she returned huskily. Moving her eyes from the bright amusement of his, she stared down at the parcel, one hand moving to tentatively explore the shape and texture. 'I didn't buy you anything,' she explained awkwardly. 'Well, I mean, I have a present for you, but——'

'But it was for someone else and you're giving it to me because you didn't have anything,' he teased, and when she nodded awkwardly, he leant over and gently squeezed her hand. 'You're giving me something better than a present,' he said easily. 'A family Christmas,' and she gave him a grateful smile. He might not mean it, in fact she didn't suppose he did, but it had been kind of him to ease the awkward moment.

'Were you intending to spend Christmas here alone?' she asked as she began unwrapping her present.

'Yes,' he admitted with a slight shrug. 'Christmas doesn't mean very much when you're on your own.'

'But you must have friends...'

'Sure——' Getting to his feet, he reproved, 'Don't let your tea get cold. I'll tell Robbie he can come in now, hm?'

'Yes. And Devlin—thank you,' she said softly.

'Pleasure. By the way,' he added with a wide smile, 'Robbie was somewhat startled by the smallness of the hoofprints. Reindeer, he assured me, have big feet!'

'Oh, dear,' she gurgled. 'What did you tell him?'

'That they were on tiptoe, of course.'

Laughing, Sam threw her pillow at him.

* * *

After she had exclaimed over Robbie's presents, had him exclaim over the enormous box of chocolates Devlin had given her, washed, dressed in a soft wool dress of sage-green that deepened the colour of her eyes, brightened her hair, she carefully made up her face in honour of the occasion. Then she smiled to herself for the small lie. She was dressing up for Devlin—and herself. It had nothing whatever to do with its being Christmas.

It was a good day, the memory of which would remain with Sam for a long time, something bright to look back on in the gloomy months ahead. As she had known, or suspected, Robbie and Devlin spent most of the day playing with the train set, and as she watched them, a hard lump formed in her throat. They looked right together, even if they didn't look very much alike, and the thought frightened her. A feeling of being edged out, of the foundations she had built beginning to shiver.

By five, Robbie could hardly keep his eyes open, and with a smile Sam took him up to bed.

'Sit,' Devlin commanded when she came back down. 'You've done enough for one day. I'm quite capable of getting us a sandwich and a cup of tea. Put your feet up. It was a lovely day, Sam—thank you.' With a rather wicked smile, he bent and kissed her mouth.

They spent the evening sitting companionably on the sofa listening to the radio, idly talking. He told her a little about his life in Canada, she told him of her life before Julie had been taken ill, and when she was in bed she lay for a while, hands tucked beneath her head going over the day. She felt warm and happy—and contented, her feelings of inade-

quacy pushed to one side, and, for the first time
since Julie had died, almost complete.

Boxing Day was the same, a good, happy day
without argument or dissension. Whether Devlin
was being careful not to introduce a jarring note,
she didn't know; she was only grateful that none
was introduced. They went for a walk in the after-
noon, behaved childishly, threw snowballs at each
other, dragged Robbie on a makeshift sledge and
as they walked home, Sam's arm tucked into
Devlin's, she consciously admitted how nice it was
to have him there. How nice it could be if he stayed.
Turning to look at Robbie, at his happy, glowing
face, she thought how much he would benefit from
being part of a normal happy family. A mother and
father, a brother or sister, perhaps. Devlin looked
happy too. Did his thoughts run along similar lines
to her own?

When she got up in the morning, it became quite
obvious that Devlin's thoughts hadn't been doing
any such thing. Sam had first noticed that the snow-
ploughs had been through, cleared the main roads,
and the second was Devlin. He was standing at the
lounge window staring out, his face moody, the
closeness she had felt with him, and thought he had
felt too, all gone. As he became aware of her, he
turned, his face once more the indifferent mask he
had worn when he had first arrived, and she knew
what he was going to say before he made his blunt
announcement.

'I've decided to go to Spain, supervise the bridge.'

'When?'

'Today.'

She didn't ask him why. She knew why. He had
pretended, and pretended very well over the past

few days, for Robbie's sake. But by his own
confession, he was a loner, he didn't need other
people; domestic bliss was not his scene. She hadn't
wanted him here, yet now that he was going, wanted
to leave, she wanted him to stay. Not trusting herself
to speak, she nodded. All the pleasure she had felt
when she woke turned to a hard, heavy weight in
her chest.

'Can you run me into Rye?' asked Devlin.

'Yes, of course,' she managed evenly. 'How soon
do you want to leave?'

'As soon as possible. There's no point in putting
it off, is there?' he asked flatly, yet his eyes searched
hers as though trying to find a message,
confirmation.

Puzzled, Sam wondered what it was he was trying
to convey. Regret? Yet why should he feel regretful?
He would have gone eventually, she knew that. Or
she and Robbie would have done. Did he realise
how much she had enjoyed his company and was
afraid she would now try to make a claim on him?
Was that it? 'No, there's no point in putting it off,'
she agreed.

'And it's what you want. Isn't it, Sam? For me
to go, leave you in peace?'

Pride should dictate that she confirm it, in fact
she thought she was going to confirm it, until she
found herself giving a little shake of her head. 'You
said . . .' she began huskily, then sighed. She had no
right to ask him to stay—and he didn't want to.
Perhaps he just wanted her to make it easy for him.
'I'll go and see if the car will start.'

'It will,' he said almost brusquely. 'I've already
cleared the snow away from it and started it up. It

seems fine. I'll get Robbie up and tell him—why don't you go and have your breakfast?'

Nodding, her face stiff, she turned away and walked heavily into the kitchen. Robbie didn't look any happier at the prospect of Devlin leaving when he joined her than she did. His eyes were red where he had been crying and he only played with his porridge, stirring it round and round his dish. She didn't have the heart to reprimand him—she hadn't been able to eat her own either, and for a moment she almost hated Devlin, for disrupting their lives so, giving them dreams that had no hope of fulfilment.

The drive into the town seemed to go far too quickly. There was hardly any traffic, nobody about much. Driving into the station yard, Sam waited while Devlin went to make enquiries. When he came back, she stared at his tall striding figure, the oddly coloured hair ruffled by the chill wind, trying, she supposed, to imprint him on her memory. She had a feeling they would not meet again, and that hurt, unbearably.

'There's a train in half an hour. Don't wait, Sam—and for God's sake stop looking as though you'd been beaten!' he snapped angrily. 'I'll let you know my address as soon as I can, if there's any problem, or either of you need anything, you'll be able to contact me there! Let me know anyway when you move, when you go back to London. I'll need a note of your bank account number, I'll get mine to transfer funds—for Robbie,' he added flatly when Sam opened her mouth to argue.

'All right,' she agreed miserably, but she didn't think she would. 'I'll get your bag from the boot.'

Removing the key from the ignition, she got out and went round to the back, leaving him to say goodbye to Robbie. Slamming the boot with unnecessary force, she handed him his bag, then they just stood and stared at each other, Sam shivering slightly in the cold.

'You'll be all right?' Devlin asked brusquely.

'Yes.'

'It's best this way.'

'Yes.'

'Oh, dammit, Sam!' he said angrily. 'I can't stay!'

'No.'

Dropping his bag with a thud, he dragged her unprotesting into his arms and kissed her hard, almost brutally, his mouth grinding her lips against her teeth. Wrapping her arms round him, she hugged him tight for a moment before he thrust her away, picked up his bag, and strode off.

'Bye,' she whispered.

Brushing impatiently at her wet eyes, Sam climbed back into the car and noisily revved the engine. Swinging out of the car park, she almost lost control as the tyres hit a patch of ice, and she hastily slowed. As Devlin had said, it was best that he go. Robbie was silent on the drive back, for which Sam was grateful; she didn't think she could have coped with questions about this or that. He didn't even ask her why Devlin had to go, just sat hunched miserably on the back seat.

He didn't eat any of his dinner, nor any of his tea, and by six o'clock Sam finally admitted to herself that his silence and flushed face were not entirely due to Devlin's leaving. Touching a hand to his forehead, she found it burning up, and her heart sank. Maybe it was just a chill from playing in the snow. Maybe he was sickening for measles or something.

Giving him two junior Disprin, she tucked him up in bed, then stayed with him until he fell into a fitful sleep. Worried, Sam remade up the camp-bed so that she could sleep beside him, just in case, and then was glad she had. He kept her awake half the night, grizzling and miserable, obviously in some discomfort, and as soon as it was light she wrapped him in his warmest clothes and drove the fifteen miles to the nearest hospital.

'Virus,' they said. 'A lot of nasty bugs going round this time of year.' They would keep him in, just in case. Had she brought any night clothes for him?

'No,' she'd had to confess. She would go back and get them, and his favourite teddy.

The next two days were a nightmare as Robbie lapsed in and out of consciousness. Sam had rung the Gunners from the hospital to explain why she wasn't at home in case they should worry about her. They'd promised to light the Aga, keep the water hot, just in case the pipes froze. Was there anything they could do? No, she had explained. It was just a matter of waiting for the antibiotics to work.

She didn't leave him, and spent most of her time sitting beside his bed, his hot little hand held in hers. He was in a side room, so she didn't even have the distraction of watching other people, other children. She'd read to him, even though she wasn't altogether sure he could hear her, or even know she was there. She'd read the hospital magazine from cover to cover, taking in not one word. She had read Robbie's chart, discovered idly and without particular interest that his blood group was different from Julie's. She had known Julie's was the same as hers, because they'd both been blood donors together. Probably Robbie had the same blood group as Devlin; she vaguely seemed to remember reading somewhere that a child must have a blood group the same as one of the parents. Not that it mattered, it was just something that flittered in and out of her mind as she sat beside him. She'd gone past mere tiredness, she now felt almost comatose, her eyes blank, unfocused, her body slumped in the chair.

'Why don't you go home, Miss Martin? You're not doing yourself or Robbie any good. We'll look after him, you know,' the sister said in exasperation, as she'd said many times before.

'I know. It's just that I feel so responsible,' Sam murmured miserably.

'Now that's just silly,' Sister reproved. 'You'll need to be alert and bright when he's up and about again, not a zombie. Why not go home and get some rest? Come back tomorrow. We have your neighbour's telephone number if we need to get in touch—not that we anticipate it!' she added hastily when Sam looked alarmed. 'We just have to wait for the virus to run its course. Now go on, away with you. And if you'll take my advice, get a taxi; you shouldn't be driving when you're so tired.'

'All right,' Sam said listlessly. Getting to her feet, she stared down at Robbie for a moment, her eyes blurred with tears. He looked so little.

CHAPTER FIVE

As SAM reached out to the door, it opened, and she just stared, her tired mind unable for the moment to differentiate between real and imagined.

'Devlin?' she whispered. 'Oh, Devlin!' Grasping the lapels of his thick coat, she buried her face against him and burst into tears. His arms were strong and comforting, and she couldn't think of anyone she'd rather have hold her at that moment than him. Holding him tightly, she gave in to her need for release from tension and worry. She was aware of a whispered conversation going on over her head, of Devlin's strong arms tightening, and then he was leading her out, along the corridor, into the lift. A large clean hanky was thrust into her hands and she blew her nose hard, trying to get her shuddering breath under control. She didn't know why he was there, she didn't care. She was just grateful that he was, someone capable and strong, someone to share the responsibility.

Leaning back against the lift wall, her face white and tired, her eyes red-rimmed, she stared at him, taking in the air of strain, the frown on his strong face, the shaggy hair that straggled across his collar, and she wanted to put out a hand to touch it, touch him, burrow back against that hard chest, be held in strong arms. When Devlin removed his frowning gaze from the indicator light above the lift doors and glanced at her, she found she didn't know what to say. She was afraid to ask why he was there.

Pushing her tumbled hair away from her face with a hand that shook, she mumbled thickly, 'I'm sorry, I——'

'Don't,' he cautioned, putting out a gentle hand to touch her face, then pull her into his arms again. 'Don't talk. The Gunners told me what had happened and I saw the doctor before I came into the ward. Robbie's going to be fine, Sam.'

'Yes,' she whispered. Anything else didn't bear thinking about. When the lift doors opened, Devlin led her out and into the grounds towards a Range Rover parked beside her Escort.

'We can collect your car tomorrow,' he told her as he opened the door and helped her inside.

Collapsing on to the leather upholstery with a tired sigh, Sam closed her eyes. It was sufficient for the moment to know he was there, would take charge. She couldn't think any more, felt quite unable to make even simple decisions. The journey took no more than twenty minutes, and when they reached the cottage, Devlin helped her out and ushered her inside.

'The kitchen will be warm,' she whispered, leading the way. 'David kept the Aga going for me.'

Without answering Devlin removed her coat, sat her down to remove her boots, then gently chafed her cold feet. 'Better?' he asked, sitting back on his heels.

'Yes.' Staring at him, her eyelids heavy, she tried to smile. 'Thank you.'

With a deep sigh, he straightened, then helped her to her feet. 'Come on, upstairs. Go and get into bed, and I'll make a hot drink.'

Dragging herself wearily up to her room, she swayed, then with a tired sigh slumped like a rag doll across the quilt. It was too much of an effort to get undressed, have a wash. She'd lie here for a minute, gather her energy, then get into bed properly.

She slept like a log until gone eleven the next morning, and when she finally opened her eyes, it was to find Devlin sitting beside her, his unusual eyes fixed steadily on her face.

'How do you feel?' he asked quietly. Not the quietness of concern, but more of indifference, and she frowned.

'I'm all right. Robbie——'

'Robbie's fine,' he said quickly, impatiently almost. 'I rang the hospital from the Gunners' early this morning. His fever's down a bit and he spent a quiet night. I brought you a cup of tea,' he added, indicating the cup sitting on the bedside table.

Hoisting herself up on the pillow, still trying to come to terms with the fact that he was there, Sam only then realised that she was in her nightdress, and she frowned. She had no memory of getting undressed, barely any memory of anything except meeting Devlin at the hospital.

'You didn't,' he told her, correctly interpreting her puzzled glance. 'I did. When I came up with your drink last night, you were out like a light. I undressed you and put you to bed.'

'Oh,' she murmured, not even able to dredge up any embarrassment. 'Thank you.' Picking up her tea, she took a few sips as she tried to work out why Devlin was different. Gone entirely was the man she had come to know over Christmas. He was back to the hard stranger, indifferent, impatient, and she felt a hollow pain inside her. Why had he come? Not because he missed her,

obviously, or liked her. 'Why are you here?' she
asked quietly. 'I thought you were going to Spain.'

'I was,' he explained flatly. 'Did. I got halfway
across to Santander before...' With a little shrug,
a mere twitch of his shoulders, he added, 'Before
deciding I couldn't do it—couldn't leave you to cope
with Robbie alone. As soon as the ferry docked, I
made arrangements to fly back. I hired the Rover
at the airport—and here I am. I've had a lot of
time to think during the past few days, and there's
really a very simple solution.'

'Is there?' asked Sam, finally raising her eyes to
his still face. 'What?' He looked tired, his hair
longer than she remembered it, his jaw more square.
The trauma of Robbie's illness, her worry and
tiredness, had made her forget his aura of power,
his strength. His arrogance. Staring at him, she
remembered their parting at the station, and
shivered. Was he remembering it too? He'd been
angry—more with himself than with her. Was that
why he'd come back? Because he thought he had
to pay?

Propping his feet on the edge of the bed, he
picked up her jar of moisturiser and began tossing
it idly between his hands. His eyes on what he was
doing, he said casually, 'We get married.'

'We get married?' she queried blankly.

'Yes, married,' he said. 'And before you go
through all the reasons why it's ridiculous, just
listen——'

'But it is ridiculous!' protested Sam, her face
startled, her eyes wide with shock. 'We barely know
each other...'

'Then we'll get to know each other!' he said
impatiently.

'Oh, fine,' she snapped, resorting to sarcasm because she was bewildered and confused, and because she wanted him to be nice to her, and he wasn't. 'What happened to the live loose unencumbered bit?'

'I might have known you'd bring that up,' Devlin muttered disagreeably. Tossing the pot on to the bed, he got to his feet and went to stand at the window, his back to her, hands shoved into his pockets. 'All I said before still stands—but I can't walk away, Sam,' he added quietly. 'Much as I want to, I can't. I have no emotional ties...'

'Except presumably for the loose attachment,' she couldn't resist taunting. 'What happened to her? Relegated to the ranks, was she?'

'She's none of your business.'

'She would be if we married,' she pointed out tartly.

'Sam,' he warned quietly, 'just shut up and listen.'

Plonking her cup down, she folded her arms and watched him, her beautiful eyes over-bright. Don't be a martyr to the cause, he'd told her once, don't make it a shrine at which you worship. Now he was doing the very thing he'd told her not to do. Why? Did he know for sure that Robbie was his son? Had he found out that his blood group was the same as the boy's? Was that what he'd talked to the doctor about the previous night? Because she clearly remembered that he'd said he'd spoken to the doctor. Frowning, barely listening to his words, she snapped to attention when he roared at her.

'Sam!'

'What? Oh, sorry, I was thinking.'

'Well, don't,' he reproved irritably. 'And don't look at me like that either, just keep an open mind until I've explained. I've thought it all out. I shall sell up here, which I intended to do anyway. I have enough for us to live reasonably well on until I decide what I want to do——'

'What about the job in Spain?'

'I've handed it over to someone else—and please stop interrupting. There's the house just outside Hastings that Nathan left me,' he resumed. 'It's a grand place for a boy to be brought up...'

'Is it also a grand place for me to live?' she asked with soft sarcasm. 'Seems to me the advantages are all on your side. You get to live where you want, get someone to take care of Robbie—what do I get, Devlin?'

'You can work if you want to—as I said, Hastings isn't far away. You get to be free from worry, financial burdens—and a man in your bed to ease the frustration that's eating away at you,' he tacked on hatefully as he turned to survey her outraged face.

'The what?' she exclaimed, sheer astonishment robbing her of coherent thought for a few moments.

'Frustration,' he repeated helpfully.

'Oh, very funny,' she retorted, pulling a face of disgust. 'Why don't you just get out of here, and take your damned stupid proposal with you?' Her mouth tight, she threw back the covers and went to collect clean clothes from the wardrobe. 'I'm going to have a wash and get dressed, and then I'm going to see Robbie.'

'Stupid?' he asked softly, walking to stand in front of her.

'Yes, stupid! We barely know each other, for one thing. I'm not sure I even like you, for another! And for the third, I am not frustrated!' Stepping round him, her eyes stormy, Sam reached the door. 'And even if I were,' she couldn't resist adding, 'you'd be the last man I'd invite to relieve it!' Tugging open the door, she had it slammed shut in her face. Swinging round, she found Devlin a great deal closer than she either expected or wanted. In fact he was standing as close as it was possible for anyone to get without actually touching her. And it frightened the life out of her—because she wanted to touch him, she thought incoherently, have him smile at her, not make this cold-blooded declaration.

Placing one hand either side of her head, he smiled nastily down into her mutinous face. 'Those considerations aside, what else is stupid about it?' he asked—oh, so reasonably.

'Everything!' she snapped. 'You're arrogant——'

'True,' he agreed softly.

'Bloody-minded!' she gritted, and as he opened his mouth, presumably to agree again, she rushed on, 'By your own admission you ride roughshod over everyone—nice life I'm likely to have, aren't I? Well, let me tell you, Devlin Howe, I'm not so damned hard up I'd take you to my bed!'

'Wouldn't you?' he taunted. 'You want me as much as I'm beginning to want you.'

'I do not! I've never wanted you!'

'Haven't you?' he asked in patent disbelief. 'What about Christmas Eve?'

'That was different! You said so yourself. We were tired, tense, I was taken by surprise...'

Moving his hand, Devlin deliberately trailed one finger down her cheek, making her jerk away and slap irritably at his hand. 'You aren't taken by surprise now, Sam,' he pointed out softly.

'No! Neither am I responding!'

'Aren't you? Then why flinch?'

'Because I don't like you! Because I don't like to be touched! Not because I'm aware of you! And let me tell you,' she practically screamed when he only looked amused, 'the only way I'd let a man in my bed is if I loved him and he loved me!'

'Love?' he derided with a little sneer that made her want to hit him. 'A euphemism dreamed up by women to cloak their desires, make it seem respectable. There's no such thing as love. There's desire, need, want...'

'I don't even know why I'm bothering to argue with you!' she burst out agitatedly. 'I have no intention of marrying you! The whole idea is too ludicrous for words!'

'No, it isn't,' he denied softly. 'Admittedly I've had longer to think about it than you, and maybe now is not the best time to broach the subject——'

'You're damned right it isn't!'

'But having broached it,' he continued evenly, 'we might as well thrash it out. Tell me your other reasons for refusing.'

'They're too numerous to mention,' she derided, her mind infuriatingly empty of even one, because all she could consider was his statement about love not existing. And why that should matter when she had no intention of marrying him anyway, she didn't know. Her nerves at screaming-point, she turned away and began rattling futilely at the door knob. 'Will you let go of the damned door?' she yelled.

'No. And this is the real Sam, isn't it?' he asked quietly, as she swung frustratedly back to face him. 'Flushed cheeks, bright eyes, temper—the way you were when I first came. Not the beautiful subdued doll you became, which I found very odd. In my experience, beautiful women are rarely the shy, retiring creatures you'd have me believe they were.'

'I'm neither shy nor retiring,' she denied, forcing the words out between clenched teeth. 'I will, however, believe that you're experienced!'

'Wise of you,' he applauded with infuriating condescension.

'You're enjoying this, aren't you?' she demanded. 'Having a whale of a time at my expense!'

'Mm, I cannot tell a lie. You really do look quite magnificent when you're angry!'

Snorting, she muttered, 'Hackneyed, Devlin— distinctly hackneyed! That line went out with Clark Gable!'

'But true, sweetheart. True. It's time to come back to the real world, Sam. I know you've had a traumatic three months—Julie dying, Peter leaving——'

'Paul!' she corrected between her teeth. 'And he has not left! I told you he wants to see me——'

'Irrelevant,' said Devlin dismissively. 'He wouldn't put up with Robbie once, he's not likely to do so again.'

'You don't know that!'

'Neither do you,' he pointed out mildly. 'No, Sam, I shouldn't pin your hopes to that particular mast, and wallowing down here won't——'

'I am not wallowing! And in a few months, when we move to London, life will be just fine! Now go away and let me get dressed!'

'Prove it,' he ordered quietly.

'Prove what? That I'll have a fine life in London?'

'No—that you're indifferent to me.'

'Oh, no. Oh, no, Devlin, I'm not that stupid!'

'Stupid?' he queried, transferring his weight to his outstretched arms, bringing him yet closer. 'What's stupid about it? Prove your indifference, and I'll leave—make financial provision for Robbie, and leave. I would have thought, for your own peace of mind, it was an eminently sensible thing to do.'

'You don't give two hoots about my peace of mind! And I doubt you've ever been eminently sensible in your entire life!' she retorted, feeling as though she were on quicksand, and the only way to get out of this in one piece was to head him off—and quickly. 'Devlin,' she began, her tone reasonable, 'I don't know what prompted this—chivalrous attitude—but you can't seriously expect me to believe that you of all people, a self-confessed loner, would want to encumber himself with a wife and child. Marriages of convenience went out with the bustle...'

'On the contrary, Miss Martin, they never went out at all. Marriages of convenience are contracted all the time. For money, property, any number of reasons.'

'But none of those applies to you,' she argued, her reasonable tone slipping slightly.

'No,' he agreed easily. 'But then I think you're missing the point, Sam. None of my proposals was for our gain, but for Robbie's. I got to thinking on the long ferry crossing, about my childhood, my early years. Remembered all sorts of things that I'd forgotten. The taunts from other children. Bastard being only one of the minor ones...'

'But that doesn't apply any more,' she said helplessly. 'There are thousands of one-parent families...'

'I know. And for the parents, mothers, fathers, that presumably is just fine. Did anyone ever ask the children how they felt? Did they, Sam? We call it progress and free living, the right to do as one chooses—but did anyone ever ask the children?'

Turning her face away, Sam bit her lip. His words were much along the same lines as she herself had put forward when Julie had insisted she keep Robbie. And although she could never, would never, deny a mother the right to keep her child, if there was a chance to rectify things, give a normal, happy family life, shouldn't it be grasped? Oh, damn him, she thought, she had enough problems without him giving her more. But she couldn't marry him; she'd never cope with someone like him.

'It could be a good life, Sam,' Devlin continued persuasively, one hand moving to touch her hair at her nape, making her give an involuntary shiver. 'He could have a pony.'

'Pony?' she asked blankly. What did a pony have to do with anything?

'Mm, maybe we could breed horses,' he continued reflectively as his hand continued to play havoc with her senses. 'There's plenty of ground at the house. Start a market garden——'

'Devlin!' she exclaimed helplessly, then hastily grabbed his hand as it began to untie the front fastening of her nightdress. 'Stop that! You're being ridiculous. You said yourself you didn't want encumbrances...'

'I didn't,' he admitted quietly, his eyes serious for once, 'but I got to thinking—oh, hell, Sam, I don't know. It was Christmas, I think. I'd never experienced family life like that, and to tell you the truth, it scared the hell out of me. Only I also enjoyed it. Enjoyed your company—and Robbie's. He's a nice little boy—and I suppose there's guilt too, for the way I behaved with Julie... It could be good, Sam, as good as any couples get out of marriage. Despite your denials, you aren't indifferent to me. Are you?'

'No,' she admitted grudgingly. Staring up at him, at the persuasion in his eyes, she felt warmth spread through her, excitement whisper along her veins, heating her blood, making her heart race.

'No. No more than I am to you,' he returned quietly. His voice was huskier, thicker, and she felt as helpless as a rag doll as he gently removed the bundle of clothes from her arms and tossed them behind him on to the bed. His unusual eyes were mesmerising, robbing her of thought, will, as he moved his eyes to her mouth. Doing the same, Sam noted how full his lower lip was, giving a sensuous look to an otherwise stern face. She remembered the feel of that mouth moving urgently on hers, the powerful arms that had held her—and the nights had sometimes been so long, so empty. His mouth was no more than an inch or two away from hers, and she wanted to close the gap, give in. It would solve so many problems...

Taking a fierce, shuddering breath, she returned her eyes to his, determined to be sensible. It was crazy to even consider that they could make a go of marriage, crazy to consider that the easing of her burdens was a basis for tying herself up to this man. Emerald and gold, she thought inconsequentially as she stared into his eyes. What colour eyes would children of their union have? And that thought was swiftly followed by another, one not so palatable, and she frowned. Julie had had blue eyes, Devlin's were gold, yet Robbie's eyes were brown—dark, almost black.

'Kiss me, Sam,' he demanded softly, sending her thoughts winging in an entirely different direction. 'Kiss me the way you were meant to kiss a man— softly, and with passion. Gently, and with hunger. Hair the colour of beechnuts doesn't denote a gentle nature. Eyes as wickedly green as Delilah don't denote compromise. So kiss me, Sam, and I'll show you a world you never dreamed existed.'

'No,' she whispered, her voice little more than a groan. Shaking her head weakly as though to enforce her half-hearted denial, she gasped as he swayed towards her and felt his warm breath feather across her parted lips. She closed her eyes and a shiver of anticipation went through her as his mouth completed the descent, warm and dry and parted. Her arms pressed back against the door behind her, fingers clenched, she allowed him to kiss her. One kiss wouldn't make any difference, would it?

Gently at first, with slow expertise, he sought a response, and when he had found it, when her mouth clung warmly to his, he used it. Like the expert he had said he was, he moved only his mouth on hers, the complete immobility of his body more tantalising than any movement could have been, his utter stillness a spur to emotions Sam had suppressed too long. He parted her mouth yet further, touched his tongue to hers, fleetingly, flirtatiously almost, making her groan and arch closer, respond, her arms moving to hold him.

With hesitant fingertips, she touched the hollow at his nape, touched her body experimentally to his, and felt branded. Her breasts, just touching his chest, tingled almost painfully at the contact, her thighs resting against his while his mouth explored hers with a growing passion that made her insides ache, her muscles clench with a need she had so long denied.

Wanting more, wanting perhaps in some crazy way to prove that he wasn't the only one with skill, she moved her body sinuously against him, felt his breath catch and hold, felt him tense, and yet still he remained apart, goading her.

'Is this what you want, Devlin?' she asked frustratedly, angry with him, with herself. 'This? And this? And this?'

'Yes,' he growled, his arms finally moving to hold her tight against him, his mouth parting hers with an exciting savagery.

Sam gave up any thoughts she might have had of resistance. The feel of his hard thigh muscles against hers excited her, the strength of his arousal prolonged the madness, the spiralling need that was driving her until he swept her up in his arms and carried her to the bed—and she came to a very shocked awakening.

Her breathing ragged, her body hot as though with fever, she dragged her mouth from his and buried her face against his chest. 'No!' she gasped.

'Is that how it was with Peter?' Devlin demanded thickly.

'Paul,' she contradicted fiercely, her fists clenched in his shirt front. 'His name's Paul, damn you!'

'But he never made you feel like that, did he?'

'No!' she yelled. 'And by the same token I won't be used like Julie! Let me go! I can't, won't...' Thrusting him away, appalled by her uncontrolled behaviour, she scrambled to her feet, grabbed her clothes and made a bolt for the door. Shaking like a leaf, she locked herself in the bathroom. She must have been insane! She'd known, she'd always known how he would be able to make her feel. How could she have been such a fool as to let him touch her? Prove it? How could she have behaved like that? She never behaved like that—never! But she'd wanted to, her mind whispered. Ever since Devlin had arrived, she'd known. Oh, not admitted, maybe, not consciously, but it was there all the same—the temper she'd treated him to at first, the awareness and then later, over Christmas, wanting to please him, be with him, wanting him to stay. Her eyes bleak, she stared at the tiled wall. But he had been right about one thing: Paul had never elicited that sort of response, nor ever would.

'Sam?'

'Go away!' she shouted tearfully, pressing back against the door as though to physically hold him at bay.

'Don't be ridiculous! You can't hide in the bathroom for the rest of the day!'

'Forever!' she yelled back.

'It was only a kiss, for God's sake!'

'Oh, yeah, only a kiss,' she derided, her body still shaking with the intensity of it, and unbelievably she heard him laugh. 'Don't you dare laugh at me, Devlin Howe!'

'What else am I supposed to do? Cry? For goodness' sake, stop behaving like a child and come out.'

'I'm not dressed.'

'Then get dressed!' Devlin retorted in exasperation. 'I'm going downstairs to make the tea.'

Her breath held, Sam listened to his retreating footsteps, and only when she heard the kitchen door close behind him did she let it out. Oh, yeah, only a kiss. Was that the sort of response he always got? Expected? Presumably it was quite commonplace to him, she thought waspishly, a flash of temper coming to her aid. She supposed she'd now be accused of being a tease. Well, she hadn't asked him to get aroused, had she? It wasn't her fault! Her hands still shaking uncontrollably as she unwittingly recalled with awful clarity just how aroused Devlin had been, she washed and dressed. Unlocking the door, she marched defiantly downstairs and flung open the kitchen door. As he had so nastily pointed out, she couldn't hide in the bathroom forever.

'And I don't want to talk about it!' she told him forcefully, deciding attack had to be the best form of defence. 'I don't wish to discuss it, analyse it——'

'Fine,' he agreed mildly, barely glancing round from where he stood pouring out the tea. 'Would you like some toast?'

'No.'

'Then drink your tea,' he said easily, putting her cup on the kitchen table, 'then we'll go and visit Robbie.'

Feeling stupid, and gauche, Sam sat at the table and picked up her cup, her eyes lowered. 'It was your own fault!' she burst out.

'Yes,' he agreed quietly, coming to sit opposite her.

'Well, it was!' she shouted, flinging up her head to glare at him.

'Did I deny it?' he asked reasonably, one eyebrow raised. 'Drink your tea.'

'If you hadn't——'

'Sam,' he said gently, 'drink your tea.'

'I don't want to drink my bloody tea!' she shouted, scrambling agitatedly to her feet. 'I want——'

'You want to pretend it never happened? Then we'll pretend. It's wiped from my mind, OK?'

'No, it isn't OK! And stop being so reasonable!'

'Would you prefer me to be angry? Yell at you? Call you names?'

'No,' she mumbled, subsiding back into her seat. 'I never behave like that! Never... Oh, God!' Collapsing on to the table, her head on her folded arms, she burst into tears.

'Sam, Sam,' he said gently, coming round the table to smooth a gentle hand over her tumbled hair. 'You've had very little sleep for the past few nights, you've been living on your nerves. You've been worried sick about Robbie, about your future—is it so wonderful that you've gone to pieces? Behaved out of character?'

'Is that what it is?' she asked tearfully, raising her head to look at him.

'Of course it is. Now blow your nose, drink your tea, and we'll go and see Robbie.'

Nodding, taking a tissue from the box he passed her, Sam blew her nose hard, then dried her tears. 'I'm sorry,' she said miserably, giving a last sniff.

'It's all right, truly.'

'Yes. But it was your fault...' Then she gave a watery smile when he laughed. 'Well, it was.'

'I know. Teach me to play with fire, won't it?'

Play with fire? It had been a conflagration!

When they reached the hospital, it was to find that Robbie was indeed a lot better. He was awake, and, though obviously still very sleepy, he managed a smile for Sam. When he saw Devlin behind her, his smile widened and he held out one small hand to him.

'Hello, soldier, how goes it?' Devlin asked softly.

'I bin sick,' said Robbie sounding almost proud, Sam thought, her eyes suspiciously moist.

'Yes, I know, but you're better now.'

'Yes. Can I come home?'

'In a little while.'

'Will you be there?'

'Yes, I'll be there,' Devlin promised.

Nodding, quite incurious as to the whys and wherefores, Robbie smiled sleepily at Sam before his eyelids lowered and his breathing deepened.

'He'll be a bit droopy for the next few days,' the sister explained, giving Devlin an appreciative glance, which Sam found extremely irritating. 'But he's over the worst. Will you be staying for a while?'

'Yes, if we won't be in the way.'

'No, no, we're always happy for the parents to stay.' With a warm smile for Devlin, and a brief nod for Sam, the sister sailed out, and Sam stared after her, a disgruntled expression on her face.

'She seems very nice,' Devlin murmured blandly, his eyes dancing with amusement.

'Huh. I suppose you're used to women flinging themselves at your head!' she retorted tartly. 'Well, don't add me to their list!'

'I won't,' he promised, his lips twitching.

Giving him a little glare, she swung back to the door. 'If you're going to be here for a few minutes, I have a phone call I need to make.'

'Sure, take your time,' he said easily, his eyes still full of that hateful amusement.

'I will,' she agreed loftily. Going out, she gave the door a little bang.

She'd decided on the drive in, with Devlin being hatefully understanding, that she would ring Paul, find out exactly why he wanted to see her. Devlin might dismiss him with a shrug, but Sam couldn't. Neither did she want to, she told herself staunchly. She loved Paul! He was everything Devlin wasn't. Kind, understanding... Well, maybe not understanding, and probably not very kind—but he was worth ten of Devlin Howe!

Standing in the long, overheated corridor, she piled some ten pences on the top of the ledge and swiftly punched out Paul's office number. She would show the arrogant Devlin Howe he wasn't the only fish in the sea! Expecting her to leap into bed with him after only knowing him five minutes! Huh! What did he think she was? Well, she wasn't that desperate for male company! Then she blushed scarlet as she remembered that hateful scene in the bedroom. If that hadn't been desperate, she'd like to know what was.

'Paul?' she asked quickly, as she heard the deep, remembered voice. 'It's Sam. Yes, yes, I'm fine,' she said impatiently when he continued to waste precious time in incidentals. 'Yes, yes, the snow's almost gone—yes, I realised that was why you couldn't come, that's why I'm ringing. Why did you want to see me?' she asked bluntly.

Coiling the phone lead round and round her finger while she listened, she nodded and shook her head in time to his statements, in no way surprised by what he was saying. 'No, Paul,' she denied quietly when he paused long enough for her to speak, 'I didn't come to my senses. No, I realise that. Goodbye.' Without waiting for him to finish, to expostulate, exclaim over her selfishness, she replaced the receiver with a quiet click. Had he always been that pompous? Yes, she supposed he had, and she couldn't believe the feeling of relief that swept over her at the knowledge that he no longer had the power to hurt her. Be it on your own head, he'd said. Well, it was, wasn't it? Had he really expected her to be at breaking-point? Rush thankfully into his arms and to hell with Robbie?

'Are you all right, dear?'

'What?' Swinging round, she stared at a plump coloured lady in a lilac overall. 'Oh, yes—yes, I'm fine, thank you.'

'Well, you surely don't look it,' the lady decided, giving Sam a wide, friendly smile. 'You look as though you could do with a drink!'

'Yes. Got a bar here?' Sam asked humorously.

'Now you know we ain't!' the woman declared in a patently false West Indian accent. With an infectious chuckle, she pointed along the corridor. 'Coffee shop's along there on the right.'

'Thank you, I'd best have coffee, then, hadn't I?' Smiling, feeling almost reprieved, Sam walked along to the little shop.

Three months ago, she thought idly as she sipped her coffee, she'd been going to marry Paul—and if he'd asked her now, agreed to have Robbie, begged, she knew she would have refused. Devlin, who had never professed to love her, or even like her, treated her better than Paul. With a long sigh, she stared down into her cup. Trying to conjure up a mental image of him, all she could see was Devlin. Rubbing her fingers over her aching temples, she wondered if she'd always been fickle. If she'd been truly, deeply in love with Paul, she would have been broken-hearted when he'd left, wouldn't she? And when Devlin had left and she'd thought she would never see him again... Groaning, she pressed her hands over her eyes, trying to shut out thoughts that wouldn't go away.

'Sam? You OK?'

Heaving a big sorry-for-herself sigh, Sam looked up at him. 'Yes,' she agreed tiredly. 'Can't escape from you, can I? Sorry, I didn't mean that as it sounded,' she apologised when he frowned and looked awkward for a moment. 'Just thoughts, Devlin, just thoughts. Robbie asleep?'

'Mm. You were gone so long I was beginning to worry.'

'Sorry. Do you want a coffee?'

'Yes, I'll get it.' Turning away, he went to the counter, and Sam watched him, examined him. She notice the way the elderly helper behind the counter smiled at him, and sighed. Age was no barrier to attraction; and he was attractive, too damned attractive.

When he returned and sat opposite her, she looked down and began stirring the remains of her coffee. 'I rang Paul,' she said quietly.

'And?' he asked equally quietly.

'And nothing.' Dropping her spoon into her saucer with a little clatter, she looked up at him, her face wan and tired. 'He wanted to know if I'd come to my senses.'

'And have you?'

'No.' Giving a little unamused laugh, Sam returned her attention to her cup. 'Daft, isn't it? All those months thinking myself hard done by, being miserable, and now I don't think I ever wanted him at all.' Looking up, her eyes almost blank as she stared at him, she asked worriedly, 'Did I choose Robbie for all the wrong reasons? Was he just an excuse to break my engagement? And yet I'm sure I didn't think that at the time. I know I didn't,' she added, frowning. 'Yet talking to Paul just now, I felt—indifferent. That's terrible, isn't it?' she asked, focusing back on his still face.

'No, not terrible. All it means is that you've changed, become a different person, with different values, different goals. You're also tired, confused, worried. The mind can only cope with one problem at a time—something I should have remembered,' added Devlin with a wry smile.

'He didn't even want to know how Robbie was,' she continued as though she hadn't heard him. 'I told him I was at the hospital... He didn't even ask what was wrong with him.'

'No. Have you finished that?' he asked, indicating her cup.

'Yes. It's cold,' she said absently, pushing the cup away.

'Come on, then,' he instructed, getting to his feet and holding her chair.

'Where are we going? Back to the ward?'

'No. We're going out to have some lunch. Robbie won't wake for a while yet, we can come back this evening. You've had enough of hospitals for the time being. We'll go for a drive, get some fresh air.'

More than happy to have someone do her thinking for her, Sam accompanied him outside.

They stopped at a country pub for lunch and she managed to eat most of the steak and kidney pie he ordered for her. Devlin had a pint and she a gin and tonic before they returned to the car. She didn't take any notice at first of where they were driving, her thoughts continued to revolve around Paul and her odd behaviour. Thinking back, she supposed she'd expected Paul to love Robbie as she did, and when he hadn't the choice had been, not exactly easy, but a foregone conclusion. The simple fact was that Robbie was more important than Paul— so why hadn't she seen that before?

It wasn't until they stopped and Devlin pulled on the handbrake that she looked up. 'Where are we?' she asked in surprise as she started in some bewilderment at the large house in front of her. Turning her head, she stared at what looked like a barn off to her left before returning her gaze to Devlin.

'Nathan's house. Or, to be more precise, mine,' he explained simply. 'Want to have a look around?' Without giving her time to answer, he climbed out and walked round to open her door.

'It's old, isn't it?' she asked lamely as she stared up at the stone frontage. It was a square house, five windows staring blindly down at them—three along the top, one either side of the heavy and old-looking front door.

'Mm, built in 1758. It needs quite a bit of work done to it. Come on.' Taking her elbow, Devlin escorted her across the patchy gravel that had dead-looking weeds pushing through, and up to the front door.

'Did you live here?' she asked as she stepped inside—then halted in surprise. From the outside it looked gaunt, inhospitable, yet inside even the cold couldn't dispel the feeling of welcome. A wide straight hall led to presumably the kitchen, a door on either side to the living-rooms, and a beautiful oak staircase curved gracefully up to the first floor. 'It's nice!' Sam exclaimed inadequately.

'Yes. Want to look round?' Again without waiting for her answer, Devlin began taking her on a tour of inspection.

The two front rooms were high-ceilinged, square, the furniture old, shabby for the most part, although there were one or two nice pieces. The enormous kitchen had been modernised with fitted wooden cabinets and a rather startling red oil-fired stove.

Upstairs, there were five bedrooms and two bathrooms, and standing at the window in the room that used to belong to Devlin, Sam stared curiously round her, trying to imagine Devlin as a small child.

'How old were you when you came to live here?' she asked.

'Fourteen.'

'Fourteen?' she exclaimed, surprised. 'I thought he'd adopted you as a child?'

'No.' With an odd smile, Devlin ran his hand over the brass footrail of the single bed, then bent to remove a thread from the bare mattress. 'He caught me trying to break into the barn. I'd run away from the home, was living rough. It was raining, I was tired, cold, hungry, the barn looked a good place to sleep. Nathan would have been in his fifties then, a big man, strong. He gave me a good hiding that night, took me into the house, cleaned me up, sat me at the kitchen table and made me tell him why. No one had walloped me before.' Flicking his eyes up to hers, he gave a twisted smile. 'In the home, I was always one of the biggest, and I used my weight and strength to terrorise the others—well, maybe not terrorise,' he qualified, 'order them to do my bidding. King of the dungheap. The teachers couldn't do anything with me, so they left me alone for the most part. Oh, they lectured me on my behaviour, but no one ever laid a hand on me. That was wrong, Sam. If I'd been chastised properly I might not have turned out to be such a bastard. At first, I thought Nathan was just another do-gooder, wanted to save my soul, and I viewed him with all the contempt a fourteen-year-old is capable of. He worked me like a dog—treated me like a dog,' he added with a small reminiscent smile. 'If I was good, I was rewarded—I got fed. If I was bad, he dealt with me, and I mean dealt...'

'But why did you stay?' Sam asked, puzzled. 'And surely the social services wouldn't have allowed you to stay with a man who beat you?'

'He didn't beat me!' he protested. 'He *disciplined* me. And the social services didn't know. When Nathan applied to foster me, they came down to inspect the premises, asked me what I thought,' he said derisively, 'and I said I wanted to stay. All my life I'd been treated with indifference—well, Nathan Howe wasn't indifferent. I came to respect him, and then to love him. I applied myself to my schooling, did all sorts of things I never thought I'd do... Another soul saved.'

'And you think I'm too soft with Robbie?' Sam asked quietly, turning to look out of the window at the damp landscape. 'You think if I'm not careful he'll end up like you?'

'No. But kids need discipline, Sam, as well as kindness. They need to know the rules. If you allow him to get his own way for too long he'll think he can always do so.'

'But it's not very long since Julie died.'

'I know, and I know it sounds heartless of me to say so, but children have very short memories. Oh, I don't say he'll forget her, he won't, and he'll be sad sometimes, miss her, hate you sometimes if you tell him off, because you aren't his mother. But if you aren't careful, he may view you with the same contempt I viewed my teachers—a soft touch.'

'Which needs to be tempered with steel,' she sighed. 'You.'

'I think so. But that doesn't mean I'm right. I'm hardly an expert. I just think he deserves all we can do.'

'Which means getting married.'

'Yes.'

'And living here?'

'If you think you could. It needs a lot of work, I know...'

But it could be made beautiful, thought Sam, focusing her eyes on the view. The house wasn't overlooked at all, and yet it was hardly isolated either—rolling farmland, woods, yet no sign of the road she knew was there. A perfect place for a small boy to grow up in. But how perfect would it be for her? If she agreed, if they lived together—loved together, her mind whispered—wouldn't her personality be submerged by his? And yet, at Christmas, she hadn't felt subjugated. She'd felt warm, and special—but then Devlin had been pretending, hadn't he? If she were his wife... And why was he so insistent? Only for Robbie's sake?

Turning to look at him, searching his face for a clue to his feelings, she gave a helpless sigh. 'I don't know, Devlin. It all seems so crazy. Have you really thought it all through?'

'Yes.'

'All the implications?'

'I think so. All the arguments for and against. We're neither of us children; we have managed, on the odd occasion, to have a reasoned, intelligent discussion. You aren't indifferent to me, in fact sometimes I think you quite like me,' he added with a small, amused smile. 'You're a beautiful, desirable woman, you don't irritate me——'

'Yet,' she put in drily.

'Yet,' he agreed. 'There's the possibility, I know, that you might meet someone in the future, fall in love,' he murmured, his mouth pulling down derisively.

'Love does exist, Devlin,' she reproved softly. 'My parents have it. They've been married twenty-eight years...'

'And been blissfully happy all that time?'

'Oh, Devlin, no one is blissful all the time. They have arguments—of course they do. Unholy rows sometimes, but that doesn't mean they don't love each other.' Turning to look out of the window once more, finding it easier to think when she wasn't facing him, she asked, 'But what if I did meet someone? Fall in love? What if you do?'

'That's a bridge we'll have to cross when we reach it. I haven't met anyone to date that I'd consider the world well lost for, so the odds are that I won't. And although I know that women are more fickle——'

'They are not!' Sam denied forcefully, swinging round to face him again. 'Or certainly I'm n——' Breaking off, she gave him an irritated glance as she recalled her thoughts on just that subject in the coffee shop. 'Well, I didn't think I was,' she concluded moodily. 'Anyway, if I lived here, I'd be well isolated, wouldn't I? Not much chance of meeting anyone and falling in love. Unless it was the local farmer, or the milkman.'

'Not even them. I intend to keep you fully occupied,' Devlin taunted softly. 'No time for farmers or milkmen.' His eyes holding hers, he walked slowly towards her.

'No!' she said raggedly, retreating until her back was to the wall. 'Devlin!'

'What?' he asked innocently as he reached her and drew her resisting body firmly into his arms. Grinning down at her, he continued. 'We could be married tomorrow morning.'

'No, we...'

'Yes, we could. I went to see about a special licence when I returned to England.'

'You were so sure you could persuade me?' she asked blankly, an expression of panic in her lovely eyes.

'No, Sam, but just on the off chance that I could, I thought it best to be prepared.'

'It sounds more to me as though it's a bitter pill you think you have to swallow. Hold your nose and quickly gulp it down.'

His face thoughtful, his eyes steady on hers, an expression in them she couldn't read, Devlin agreed quietly, 'I don't say it was what I thought I wanted from my life, and I suppose your analogy has an element of truth, but I truly think it's the best solution in the circumstances. And that being so, why wait? Well?' he queried when she still looked obstinate. 'What possible reason is there for waiting? You can cable or ring your parents. It's a little late for them to get here in time, and if you really want them to be here, I can, I suppose, change the date.'

'Kind of you—if I wanted to marry you, which I didn't say I did.'

'Come on,' he chided, 'where's your sense of adventure? It won't be so bad. I promise not to beat you.'

'Hm!'

'I promise to honour and obey you...'

'Oh, very likely,' she retorted derisively. 'I bet you've never obeyed anyone in your life. Have you?'

'Only Nathan,' he admitted with a wry smile, his eyes crinkling with humour. 'But I could quite get to like obeying some of your commands,' he informed her suggestively, then laughed when she went scarlet.

'That wasn't fair! You said you wouldn't mention it again. And supposing——'

'Supposing, supposing,' he growled, staring down into her troubled face. 'Will you stop putting obstacles in the way? Why not look on the positive side?'

'Because presumably I'm not very positive!' Sam retorted crossly. 'I obviously don't have your stamina—I didn't mean that!' she exclaimed when he gave a derisive snort. 'I meant—oh, I don't know what I meant. You just seem so—well, you give off this air of restless energy, as though you're always up and doing—and I don't think I'm like that. I'm a quiet sort of person. It takes me a long time to weigh the pros and cons...'

'I'll bear it in mind,' Devlin murmured drily, 'after we're married—only I don't think you know yourself at all, Selina Anne Martin. I don't think you've ever been given the chance to find out. Green eyes and red hair, as I've said before, do not denote staidness of character.'

'I don't have red hair!'

'Reddish,' he corrected with a wicked smile. Running his fingers through the thick, shining strands, he repeated softly, 'Reddish. Say yes.'

'No.'

'Yes,' he pressed softly, with a wicked smile.

'Stop rushing me.'

'And if I stop rushing you?'

Gazing at him consideringly for a moment, her head on one side, her eyes wary, Sam said tentatively, 'If—and I only say if——' she warned hastily '—if we could take time to get to know each other properly before—well, before...'

'Consummating it, you mean?' he asked helpfully, his eyes filled with hateful amusement.

'Yes.'

'If that's what you want.'

'It is!' she said with curious insistence.

'All right.'

'You really think it's the right solution?' she asked almost pleadingly. 'For Robbie's sake?'

'Yes, Sam,' he agreed gently. 'It seems almost certain I'm his father. We have the same blood group...'

'You checked?'

'Yes. And when we've sorted ourselves out we could maybe manage a honeymoon to get to know each other properly, if Barbara and David will look after Robbie.'

Staring into his face, Sam found it curiously hard to summon up any more arguments, and if Devlin was Robbie's father, it wasn't fair to deny him, was it? 'All right, maybe—I didn't say yes!' she admonished almost frantically as he began to smile. 'I said maybe!'

CHAPTER SIX

THEY were married the following morning at eleven-thirty. Devlin looked unfamiliar and stern in a dark grey suit, Sam elegant in a navy suit and white silk shirt that she hadn't worn since she had left work. She made her responses as though she were drugged; she felt like a mechanical doll that had been wound up just enough to get her through the ceremony. David and Barbara Gunner, with surprised pleasure, had agreed to be witnesses. There was no photographer, only a few snaps taken hastily by David, who insisted that they had to have some record of the occasion. They had a celebratory lunch at a nearby hotel, then Barbara and David went home, and Devlin and Sam went to the hospital to visit Robbie before returning to the cottage.

Staring at Devlin's still face as he halted the Range Rover in the drive, Sam thought he looked about as ecstatic as she felt. Nervously twisting the new gold band on her finger, she wondered what happened next—and found out before she thought she was quite ready. Climbing out, Devlin opened her door, then swept her up in his arms.

'What are you doing?' she exclaimed, shocked.

'Carrying you over the threshold,' he said drily. 'Got your key?'

Her lips pursed, Sam found her key and awkwardly manoeuvred it into the lock, then tried futilely to struggle free when he kicked it shut behind him and carried her up the narrow staircase.

'No! Devlin, put me down! Devlin!'

With a look of wicked mockery, he carried her into her room and dumped her on the bed. Before she could move, he perched on the edge of the mattress, captured her wrists and forced them above her head.

'Devlin, this is not funny!'

'Am I laughing?' he asked softly.

'Devlin! You surely can't expect... You promised?'

'I lied.'

'But we barely know each other.'

'Then now would seem a very good time to find out. No Robbie here to disturb us...'

Staring into those golden eyes that she had once likened to a predator, Sam thought how right she had been. She felt every bit as terrified as a rabbit would be when confronted by a hawk. Nervous, and panicky, and excited, liquid warmth filling her insides. 'You're hurting my arms,' she whispered.

'No, I'm not, I'm holding you very gently—and I intend to make love to you—Mrs Howe,' he concluded softly.

Green eyes locked with yellow, she pleaded faintly, 'I need time...'

'We have all the time in the world. We don't need to go back to the hospital until this evening. Plenty of time.'

'I didn't mean that!'

'I know.' With another mocking smile, he lowered his head until his mouth just brushed hers. Without releasing her wrists, he climbed on to the bed and lowered himself on top of her.

'No,' she whispered. 'No!' Her eyes wide and fearful, she took a shaky breath and tried to hold herself rigid. Only she couldn't control her senses that accepted the warmth of him, the strength, the way his touch made her feel deep inside, the flood of desire in the pit of her stomach. She knew her eyes were darkening, could feel them do so, and strove desperately to remain immune.

'Yes,' he whispered persuasively, his face lowering until his nose touched hers.

'No!' she groaned. 'Please—no, Devlin, I'm not ready...'

'Yes, you are, I can feel your body melting, changing, as mine's changing,' he growled deep in his throat, his voice slurring, becoming husky, imperative. 'Feel, Sam, just feel...' His words smothered as his mouth captured hers, he teased her lips apart, touched his tongue to hers as he had done before, moved his body imperceptibly to accommodate her growing need.

No, her mind insisted, this is too soon, I'm not ready for this—yet her body disagreed. It seemed to flow against his and as her head fell back he released her wrists and curved warm palms to her cheeks, moving her head so that he could kiss her more easily, could range from her lips to her eyes to her neck, and she shivered as he bit gently at the cord below her ear, moved her jacket aside, began to undo the buttons of her silk shirt and slowly, so very slowly began to move his fingers up over her ribcage until they encountered the lacy barrier of her bra. Halting for barely a moment, a fraction in which he drew a ragged breath, they stole upwards until they could move the lacy barrier aside and she gave a little sobbing sound of surrender, her hips, without her conscious volition, thrusting upwards to meet his.

'So many ways, Sam,' he breathed, his mouth close to her ear, 'so many ways to make love. Let me show you, Sam—dear God, let me show you.' Moving his parted mouth across her jaw, to her cheek, he continued to whisper to her, as his hand continued to move, tease, arouse.

'It's not fair,' she groaned, moving her head agitatedly from side to side, her body hot and aching and needing. 'To make me feel like this, to make me ache so.'

'No,' he said gently, 'relax, Sam—shh, relax.' With practised movements he undid her skirt and slowly removed it, then, equally slowly, removed her jacket and blouse, and before she had time to feel the chill air on her naked skin, he began to kiss her, hands and mouth moving in a smooth, tantalising glide from her shoulder to her thigh. Removing her stockings, suspender belt, bra, and finally her lacy pants, he showed her just how many ways there were to make love.

Sam didn't know at what point he removed his own clothes, she had no memory of it at all, only the feel of his warm, smooth flesh against hers, the exciting touch of his tongue that tormented her in ways she'd only read about, never experienced. He guided her own inexperienced hands across his body, taught her all he knew, then slowly, with exquisite tenderness, he entered her, his eyes holding hers. Unable to look away, she read the passion and the need in his face, as he could see them in hers, as he had intended, and she discovered just how much more erotic it was to see, not merely to feel, imagine. Slowly, his breathing altering, growing harsh, uneven, as was hers, Devlin moved his body, gently at first, tantalisingly, the rhythm slowly building, growing, as need accelerated, became a desperate race they must both win.

Exhausted, her neck still arched in surrender, eyes now closed, Sam was surprised when he didn't move, didn't slump tiredly, or roll away, but remained still until she lifted her lashes to find him watching her.

'Aren't you glad you said yes?' he whispered provocatively.

'I don't remember that I did,' she reproved shakily, her eyes still reflecting shocked surprise at her passionate response. 'I just hope you don't live to regret it.'

'Best make sure I don't, then, lady,' he growled, his tongue flicking out to trace her mouth, 'else you'll be in big, big trouble.'

She didn't think he was entirely joking. 'I'll be in big trouble?' she asked softly, fighting to keep her voice steady, not to betray the tremors she was still feeling from his lovemaking, the feel of him still inside her, from the way a man could make her feel who didn't love her. 'I didn't insist on getting married.'

'No, but it's your job to keep me satisfied, little lady.'

Like Julie? she wanted to ask. In this same bed? 'And don't keep calling me that,' she said waspishly.

'Why? It's what you are—and I'm a man with a very big appetite.' With a slow smile that melted her against her will, Devlin finally moved, rolled to the side and hugged her against his side, her head on his shoulder, her fiery hair spread across his chest.

Moving her hand cautiously, her fingers barely touching him, she traced the hard-muscled stomach, each rib, her eyes on her task. How odd, she thought hazily, to make love to someone she barely knew. To make love to a stranger. Her fingers looked white against his tanned flesh—Paul's skin had been pale. Odious to make comparisons, yet natural, she supposed, when Paul had been the only other man to ever touch her. Yet the comparisons were all in Devlin's favour. His body was warm, fit, and large. He seemed to fill the narrow bed—and that too was exciting, because it meant they could not separate, could not move aside to sleep but must of necessity cling together to keep from falling out. There were no awkward elbows digging in, no bony chest on which to lay her face, no irritable wriggling to get comfortable.

The scent of his skin filled her nostrils, the easy rise and fall of his chest relaxing, and she curled more warmly against him, unconsciously provocative as she moved her leg across his. Mrs Howe, she thought. Selina Howe, and a small smile formed in her eyes. Making love to a stranger wasn't so bad.

'What are you thinking?' he asked quietly, his breath stirring her hair.

Moving her head, she looked down into his face and told him.

'Still a stranger, Sam?' he asked lazily, his eyes amused.

'Yes,' she said quietly, 'still a stranger.'

'But not quite so strange as I was?' he asked humorously, one dark brow arching upward.

'No.' Staring down into eagle eyes, she saw herself reflected, like a fly trapped in a spider's web, and shivered.

'What's the matter?'

'Nothing,' she denied hastily. 'I just felt a bit cold.'

'I'd best warm you up, then, hadn't I?' With a smooth, controlled movement, he scooped her to lie on top of him and dragged the covers up over her naked back. 'Make love to me, Sam,' he persuaded, his eyes intent on hers. 'Be a pity to waste all that new-found expertise, wouldn't it? I shan't expect to be the one to always make the first move.'

And that, Sam thought, sounded suspiciously like an order. And if he'd looked at those children in the home the way he was looking at her now, she didn't in the least blame them for always obeying him. Would he have spoken that way if he felt more than desire for her? His words had a mechanical sound to them, as though he had said them many times before. To other women—and it hurt. Was it only the scenery that was different? The location?

'Why are you looking at me like that?' he asked softly, his own eyes narrowing slightly.

'I was just thinking that you're a very dangerous man, Devlin Howe,' she lied. Not that it was truly a lie, but it wasn't what she'd been thinking.

'Believe it, lady, believe it,' he commanded, his eyes alight with laughter, his strong arms warm about her back, 'and you're wasting time.'

'I was being tantalising,' she quipped, suddenly throwing caution to the winds. She'd made her bed, or allowed him to do so, so she might as well enjoy lying in it, mightn't she? With a slow smile, almost as wicked as his own had been, even if it did have a tendency to wobble, she obeyed his whispered instructions. He was her husband; maybe she could teach him to feel.

* * *

They were somewhat later arriving at the hospital than they had intended. As Devlin had pointed out, he had a very large appetite. Sam had also discovered, much to her surprise, that hers matched it. Walking up to the ward, her hand tucked into Devlin's, she gave a small contented smile. Maybe things wouldn't be so bad after all. Possession was nine tenths of the law, wasn't it? And she surely had been possessed.

'If you continue to look like that,' he whispered softly, 'everyone's going to know what you've been up to.'

'I haven't been up to it on my own, though, have I?'

'No, but I don't look like the cat who swallowed the cream.'

'No, you look like the cat who ate auntie's pet budgie!'

With a warm laugh, Devlin released her hand and hugged her to his side instead. 'Some budgie!'

Yeah, she thought, some budgie. How could she have lived twenty-five years and not known herself at all? Wanton Sam, very, very wanton. Stealing a look at him, she found he was watching her, a faint smile round his mouth. Going pink, she released herself and walked into Robbie's room.

He was sitting up in bed, various toys from the main ward spread across his blankets, and he looked so much better it was hard to believe he was the same little boy of yesterday. A student nurse was leaning over the rail helping him with a jigsaw.

Looking up, he gave a wide smile that brought a lump to Sam's throat.

'Hi,' she greeted him huskily. 'You look much better.'

'Am, Sam, am,' he said with a flippancy that made her grin. 'Going home tomorrow.'

'Are you?' Glancing at the nurse for confirmation, and seeing her nod, Sam smiled. 'Good. I've been lonely without you.'

With typical male arrogance, Robbie dismissed that and turned to Devlin. ''Lo, Devlin.'

''Lo yourself.' With a relaxed grin, Devlin draped himself over the bed rail and inserted a piece into Robbie's puzzle.

They stayed for an hour, playing with him, listening to his news, answering his questions, until the sister shooed them out, wanting to settle Robbie for the night.

'You can pick him up about eleven, after doctor's rounds.'

As they walked back to the car, Sam was silent, remembering Robbie's pleasure in Devlin's easy company. He was good with the boy, neither patronising, nor overpowering. And Robbie obviously preferred his company to her own. Oh, Sam, don't be paranoiac, she scolded herself. Devlin's like another new toy, that's all. Only she had been used to Robbie's undivided attention, being the centre of his world—and now she was jealous. Dear God, what sort of person did that make her?

'Now what are you fretting about?' he asked lazily as he helped her into the car. 'Worried about telling him we're married?'

'No, not really. He likes you . . .'

'Ah.'

'What's that supposed to mean?' she asked irritably.

'You know very well what it means,' he returned gently, turning to face her in the narrow confines of the car. 'And you're being very silly.'

Staring at him, her body stiff, Sam slowly relaxed, ashamed of herself. 'I know,' she sighed. 'These last few days I've been discovering a whole lot of new things about myself—some of them not very nice.'

'But most of them pretty good,' he teased. 'I didn't promise it would be easy, Sam, there are changes all of us will have to make. You at least have a head start. You're used to a small boy disrupting your life. I'm not—and I certainly can't promise not to make mistakes. We both will.'

'I know. I think I'm only just beginning to realise what's involved. I've been used to making my own decisions—I'm not sure I'll be very good acceding to yours.'

'No,' he agreed wryly as he started the engine.

Their conversation still uppermost in her mind when they reached the cottage, Sam tried to picture just how it would be. Offset against the financial advantages, the shared responsibility of Robbie, there was also the restriction of privacy, of not being able to do what she wanted when she wanted. She didn't somehow think Devlin would alter his lifestyle—at least not to the extent of taking her wishes into consideration if he wanted to do something of his own. Yet she had the feeling that he would expect her to clear everything with him if she did. Suddenly assailed by fresh doubts, she stared blindly at Devlin as he knelt to put a match to the fire. After their conversation in the hospital car park, he too had been quiet, reflective. Was he wondering much the same things?

With a long sigh, she went to put the kettle on, and while waiting for it to boil, she stood looking through the window, elbows clasped in her palms. The sky was dark and clear, the smattering of stars bright, indifferent. The full moon threw cold light across the garden, highlighting the snowman Robbie and Devlin had built. It looked a very sorry affair now, grey and dirty. The snow surrounding it, that had looked so pretty when it fell, was now pitted and uneven. Icicles hung from the overhang above the kitchen door, and she shivered.

When Devlin's image joined hers in the window, she stared at it, as though staring at a ghost.

'Regretting it? Wishing you hadn't been so hasty?' he asked quietly, putting gentle hands on her shoulders.

'I don't know,' she whispered, giving the little quiver that his touch always produced. 'It just seems odd somehow, as though everything's out of kilter. Normally when people get married it's because they've fallen in love, want to spend the rest of their lives together. Have children...'

'You think I'd object to children?' he asked softly, his breath stirring the hair at the nape of her neck, renewing her awareness.

'Wouldn't you?'

'No, I don't think so. I hadn't really thought about it. But if you want children of your own, I don't mind.'

'Oh, Devlin, it's not a question of not minding. They'd be yours too.'

'So I should hope.'

'Oh, please don't joke about it,' she urged, swinging round in the circle of his arms. 'I feel so muddled and confused. How can I know if I'm doing the right thing?'

'It's a bit late for that. I know I rushed you, but leaving it wouldn't have made anything clearer, would it?'

'It would have given us a chance to get to know each other better.'

'Maybe,' he agreed a trifle moodily.

'I still don't really know why you were so insistent!' she exclaimed. 'After everything you said.' Perhaps if he could clarify his reasons she would find it easier to come to terms with it. 'You personally, leaving Robbie aside . . .'

'My dear girl, if we left Robbie aside, there'd be no reasons. Would there?'

'No,' she agreed on a little sigh.

Framing her unhappy face with his palms, Devlin stared down into her eyes. 'Were you perhaps hoping I'd fallen in love with you, Sam? Is that it?'

Yes, she thought, I think perhaps I was; only she couldn't tell him that, could she? When it very clearly wasn't what he wanted? Staring long and hard into his eyes, hoping perhaps to find some spark, and finding only gentle mockery, she gave a little shake of her head. 'No,' she denied, 'you made your views very clear on the question of loving. But it just seems so wrong to give myself to someone only because they don't find me an antidote——'

'Oh, Sam,' he exclaimed on a grunt of laughter, 'I didn't say that! I like you, admire you—fancy you rotten. You're very far from an antidote, as you know very well.'

'You said it would be no hardship to make love to me, as though—well, as though I were a marketable commodity!' she burst out. 'And don't laugh! I don't find it in the least amusing! Oh, Devlin, I just feel so confused! I mean, I thought I loved Paul! Yet not three months later, I feel nothing at all!'

'But you don't love me, Sam, do you?' he asked quietly, tilting her chin up so that he could see her face clearly. 'Do you, Sam?' he added with curious insistence.

'No,' she whispered, not knowing that she knew anything of the sort. She had a horrible feeling that somewhere along the way she *had* fallen in love with him. Lowering her lashes, she stared at his throat, not wanting him to see the confusion in her eyes, because he didn't want her to love him, did he? Otherwise he wouldn't have asked her so insistently, as though daring her to admit anything so foolish. So what else could she say but no?

'So, not loving me,' he continued in a flat voice that was difficult to analyse, 'you can't fall out of love. Can you?'

'No.'

'So the argument doesn't apply. Does it? And I've already told you that should you meet someone, and fall in love,' he added derisively, 'then I won't put obstacles in your way, didn't I?'

'Yes.'

'And you don't find my touch abhorrent, do you? So what other objections are there? Hm? I don't think I have any deplorable habits that are liable to drive you to drink. I shan't beat either you or Robbie. I shan't keep you short of funds—and in my own way I'll be as caring and considerate as I know how. It can work, Sam.'

With a faint smile, she looked up at him again. 'Yes, I know, if we both work at it. Perhaps I'm just making a last-ditch stand for independence...'

'And we all know what happens to last-ditch stands, don't we? I mean, look at the Battle of the Little Big Horn.'

'Oh, by all means,' she retorted acidly, 'let's look at that, but let me tell you I don't find it at all flattering to be compared to General Custer!'

Smiling, he bent to drop a light kiss on her nose. 'Oh, I don't know, he probably had the same sort of daft courage. Anyway, I refuse to divorce you after being married only one day. Now that *would* look fickle!'

With a little slap against his chest, she pushed him lightly away and went to make the tea, but her eyes were still shadowed by confusion and doubt.

At nine o'clock, after both had made a great pretence of being wholly absorbed in the play on the radio, they looked at each other, and burst out laughing.

'Never has an evening so dragged,' Devlin said wryly as he turned the radio off. 'May we go to bed now?'

'Yes. And why we had to sit here like good little children waiting until it was late enough to go up, I don't know!' Sam retorted as she switched off the light and preceded him up the stairs.

'I was being considerate,' he explained with an air of ill-usage. 'I don't want you to think I'm an animal, do I?'

'Oh, I didn't think that,' she denied, turning to glance at him as she reached the bedroom door. 'I

thought you an eagle—or a vul——' With a squeal
of laughter as he reached for her, she turned and
ran into the room.

Slowly closing the bedroom door, he grinned,
then launched himself boyishly on to the bed.
'Come here,' he ordered softly.

They picked Robbie up from the hospital the next
morning, and Devlin then drove on to Rye to put
the cottage up for sale, while Sam took Robbie
home in her own car which was still parked at the
hospital. On the way back, Sam called in at the
Gunners', partly to thank them for acting as witnesses to the wedding, and partly because she
needed another woman to talk to. For reassurance,
she supposed, that she was doing the right thing.
Although, as Devlin had pointed out, it was a bit
late to decide she wasn't.

When they got home, Sam feeling better for
having shared her worries, she sat Robbie down and
carefully explained their changed circumstances.

'Will that make him my daddy?'

'Well, yes, sort of. The same way that I'm sort
of your mummy. Not your real mummy, just
someone who looks after you, like a mummy,' she
explained, beginning to wish she hadn't embarked
on quite such a confusing explanation. It would
have been so much simpler to have said yes and
leave it at that. But she didn't want him to think
she was trying to take his real mother's place, or
that Devlin would take him away from her. She
needn't have worried. The ins and outs of parent-
hood were clearly the last thing on his mind.

'So if he's my daddy,' he continued slowly, his dark brown eyes fixed rather calculatingly on her face, she felt, 'then I can have a bike, can't I?'

'Says who?' asked Sam in astonishment.

'Peter!' he exclaimed triumphantly. 'Peter says when you have a daddy you can have big things—like a bike. So can I?'

'What a calculating little wretch you are,' she said, trying to make her expression stern and failing miserably. Here she'd been worrying herself sick as to how he would take it, and all he could think about was a bike. 'It wouldn't matter to you who your new daddy was, would it? So long as you could have a bike?'

His face thoughtful, as he presumably tried to work that out, Robbie suddenly smiled. 'I do like Devlin,' he pronounced, as though that made it all right. 'So will you ask him if I can have a bike?'

'Perhaps,' she qualified, her eyes amused. 'If you're good.'

'I'm always good.' With a wide happy grin, his energy back in full measure, he zoomed out and up to his room to check that it was all as he'd left it.

Five minutes later he was back. 'Sam?'

'Yes, darling?'

'Is Devlin going to stay with us?'

'Yes, of course.'

'He won't go away?'

'No, Robbie,' Sam comforted gently, 'he won't go away.'

'OK.' With a happy smile, he went back to his room.

*   *   *

The next few days were taken up with going through everything in the cottage, throwing out what they no longer required, packing the things that weren't of immediate need. In truth, with so much to do, any awkwardness there might have been was submerged by the chaos—not helped by Robbie, who insisted on helping. Although, Sam had to confess, Devlin was far more tolerant than she had expected. Far more tolerant than she was herself when he seemed to be underfoot every minute of the day. Boisterous, over-excited—yet usually with one word Devlin managed to check him, and that nasty niggling little jealousy rose to the surface again.

She also discovered something else about marriages of convenience. It was proving difficult to make spontaneous gestures without the worry of thinking they might be misconstrued. If they'd been a normal, loving couple, she could have teased Devlin, slipped her arms round him whenever she felt the need—and she had to admit that the need seemed quite frequent. Only she didn't know if that was what he wanted. On the other hand, when he did the same to her, she knew exactly what he wanted. Not that she didn't want it too, but she wanted it for different reasons. Loving reasons. And it hurt. Not that she didn't respond, because she did. With her own passionate nature awakened, she could do little else, nor did she really want to—she just wanted the words that would have been hers had he loved her. Words she could have said to him had he known she was falling in love with him.

Should she tell him how she was beginning to feel? No, she decided, because if he laughed, or rebuffed her, everything would be ten times worse. Perhaps it would get better when they were more used to each other. She found him watching her sometimes too, as though he were puzzled, unsure.

When they were in bed that night, both sated after their lovemaking, both lying on their backs, staring up at the ceiling, Devlin surprised her by asking, 'Is it how you thought it would be?'

Turning her head, seeing his profile outlined against the window, and wary of answering something he hadn't asked, Sam probed, 'In what way?'

'Oh, I don't know. If you thought about how it would be, does this come up to your expectations, I suppose I meant.'

'I don't know that I had any expectations,' she murmured, feeling her way. 'Or not specific ones.' Had it not come up to his expectations? Was that what he meant? Taking a deep breath, suddenly deciding that as he'd broached the subject it might be best to explain something of what was troubling her, she added hesitantly, 'I find I don't know how you want me to behave—what you want me to be. I mean, I try to do all the things you might expect a wife to do, but I don't know if that's what you want, what you were expecting.'

'No,' he agreed, giving a long sigh. Sliding his arm beneath her, pulling her warmly against his side, he put his other hand beneath his head and continued his contemplation of the ceiling. 'I don't think I know what I expected either.'

'You're disappointed?' she asked quietly, trying desperately to keep her disquiet from showing in her voice. 'Is that it?'

'No-o, not disappointed exactly, more—well, I feel as though I'm playing a part! As though the moves have all been worked out beforehand and left nothing to chance. No spontaneity...'

'You feel trapped?'

'No,' he denied slowly. 'Not trapped. Incomplete. As though something's missing.'

It is, she wanted to tell him. Feelings, those are what are missing, only she couldn't tell him that, he had to work it out for himself. But at least he was aware that something was missing, and that was a start.

'Is it my fault?' she asked carefully, her breath almost held.

'I don't know. Sam, do you feel anything for me at all? Apart from desire, from—oh, hell, sex, I suppose I mean,' he concluded impatiently. 'Do you? No, don't answer that, it's not a fair question. Don't take any notice, I'm behaving like a . . . Well, I don't know what I'm behaving like.'

Like a man who's wondering if he might have made a mistake?

Removing his arm, he rolled over to face the window. 'Goodnight, Sam.'

'Goodnight,' she whispered.

More frightened than she would have thought possible, she stared blindly in front of her, and when she was sure he was asleep she got up and went downstairs. How many years before Robbie grew up? Twelve? Thirteen? And how did you make someone fall in love with you who didn't even know he needed to? Who didn't believe it existed? And you couldn't love to order, could you? Sinking down on to the sofa, one of the cushions cuddled to her to combat the cold, and the loneliness, she felt her eyes prick with tears. What now, Sam? Become his friend? His biddable chattel? Or ask him if he wanted to leave? They could remain married, she supposed, he could support Robbie if he wanted to... Only she didn't want him to leave. She wanted him to stay, wanted it to be a real marriage.

She sat there for a long time until she was too cold to think straight, until she was shivering—and getting pneumonia wouldn't solve anything. Creeping back upstairs, she climbed carefully into the warm bed, careful not to disturb Devlin.

He was quiet the next day, answering only absently questions she or Robbie put to him, and, afraid to probe, afraid what his answer might be if she pressed him, Sam let things ride. Yet in the end, it was he who took her to task for her behaviour when she snapped at Robbie.

'Don't take it out on him, Sam,' he reproved quietly. 'He needs time to adjust too.'

'I know that, but he's behaving abominably...'

'Because he's unsure—unable to figure out how you feel, what you think. There've been a lot of changes in his young life——'

'I know that!' she snapped irritably. 'Who should know better?' Ashamed of herself, she turned away. 'I have to make the beds.'

'Sam,' Devlin said on a sigh as he halted her flight and turned her round, 'we knew it wouldn't be easy, that it would take time. Don't bottle your feelings up inside you. Share them.'

'The way you do?' she asked pointedly, giving him a defiant little glance.

'*Touché*.' With a wry smile, his distant look dispelled for the moment, he perched on the settee arm and pulled her on to his knee.

'You've barely said two words to me this morning,' she murmured, her lower lip pushed out in a pout.

Looking at her sideways, he confessed with a little grin, 'I was sulking.'

'Sulking?' she exclaimed. 'Why?'

'Because you tend to treat me like Robbie.'

'I don't!'

'Don't you?' he asked gently. 'When I try to do anything, help, I get scolded for doing it wrong, for putting something back in the wrong place. I got my head snapped off for treading dirt on the kitchen floor...'

Staring at him, recognising the truth of his words, Sam hung her head miserably. 'I'm sorry,' she whispered. 'It's because I'm unsure of myself, unsure how to behave.'

'And you think I'm not? You sometimes look at me as though you hate me. Do you? Blame me for forcing you into a marriage you didn't want?'

'No, of course not.'

'But you don't really need me, do you?' he asked with a wry twist to his mouth. 'You think I interfere where Robbie's concerned—and maybe I do. I just thought you were handling him all wrong.' Lifting her to her feet, he got up and went to stand at the window, his back to her. 'There's arrogance for you. I know absolutely nothing about children...'

'You handle him better than I do.'

'Do I?'

'Yes.' Staring at his back, needing very badly some reassurance of her own, she began hesitantly, 'I know I've been behaving erratically, up one minute, down the next, and I'm grateful that you've been so forbearing——'

'I don't want your gratitude, Sam. I want...'
Shoving his hands into his pockets, Devlin stared
down at his feet. 'Sam, what I said last night...'

'Sam, Sam, Devlin!' shouted Robbie, erupting
into the lounge. 'David's here! Can I go play with
Peter? Can I?'

What perfect timing! Always put off till
tomorrow those things you didn't want to discuss
today.

'We'll talk later,' Devlin promised wearily, yet he
sounded almost relieved not to have to talk about
it either. Taking one hand out of his pocket, he
allowed Robbie to tug him outside, while Sam
followed more slowly.

'Hello, David,' she greeted him, giving him one
of her warm smiles, albeit a trifle shaky, and didn't
see the look Devlin gave her. 'Hello, Peter.' Affectionately ruffling the gap-toothed youngster's hair,
she watched as he and Robbie raced off.

'Want to get rid of your monster?' asked David.

'Yes, please. Did you walk over?' she enquired,
surprised. 'I didn't hear the car.'

'No, Barbs has it. She needed to go into Rye. I
thought you'd be over at your house,' he added
turning to smile at Devlin.

'No, but it's an idea,' Devlin agreed without the
least vestige of warmth. 'I ought to go and make
sure the electricity has been reconnected. I'll run
you back and go on from there. I'll get my coat.'

As he turned back into the cottage, Sam stared
after him. So that they didn't have to talk any more?
she wondered.

'Is everything all right?' asked David. 'Devlin
sounds a bit fed up, and you, my dear girl, look
decidedly peaky.'

'We're OK,' she said, summoning up another shaky smile, 'it's just that there seems so much to do. Taking Robbie will be a big help. I'll pick him up later, if that's all right.'

'No need, I can run him back after tea.'

When Devlin returned a few minutes later, Sam avoided his glance, only instead of leaving immediately as she had expected she hung back until David was out of earshot. 'What's this with David?' he asked coldly.

'David?' she echoed blankly.

'Yes, David,' he mimicked. 'He obviously expected you to be on your own...'

'Why should he want me to be on my own?' she asked, thoroughly bewildered.

'Don't be obtuse!' he gritted angrily. 'And I don't intend to be long in town,' he continued silkily, 'so it would be a waste of his time to start anything when he brings Robbie back again!' Shrugging his arms into his coat, he halted at the back door for a parting shot. 'I don't share, Sam! Remember that!'

'My God, anyone would think you were jealous!' she exclaimed.

'Jealous? No. Possessive. There's a subtle difference.' Slamming the back door, Devlin walked round to start the car.

Yes, there was a subtle difference, Sam thought on a long unhappy sigh. To be jealous, you had to care. And she just wished he'd get that bee out of his bonnet about David. He couldn't honestly think—yes, he could, she thought despondently. Devlin could think any damn thing he chose—and usually did. She'd thought he'd understood that she and David were only friends, as she was with his wife, thought his previous picking about it was only done out of temper. In fact that was all it probably was now. He couldn't seriously think she and David were involved in some intrigue. You only had to see the Gunners together to know that they were crazy about each other. And she'd certainly never fancied David! She liked him, yes, but as a friend, nothing more. Although, if it provoked that sort of reaction, maybe she ought to drop David's name into the conversation more often. Possessiveness was better than indifference!

Feeling irritable and cross, she walked slowly upstairs. Now would be a good time to clear out the loft, if she could keep her mind off Devlin and his odd behaviour for long enough. Impatient with herself, she grabbed the chair from the bedroom and set it beneath the loft hatch.

After Julie had died, Sam had put all her personal belongings up there, and she had kept putting off sorting them out. With Robbie out of the way, this was an excellent opportunity. Anything she thought he might want to have of his mother's when he was older could be packed away before he came back. Clambering awkwardly up, remembering the other time when they'd been looking for the Christmas decorations, she gave a sad smile. A lifetime ago, it seemed now. Was that when she had first begun to care for Devlin? He'd been kind then, thoughtful, and those days they had spent together had been some of the happiest she'd known. How many more Christmases would they spend together? None? she wondered bleakly.

Maybe if they had children of their own... Sitting in the loft opening, Sam stared blindly into the dark shadowy corners beneath the roof. She would like to have his children, she admitted, and felt a twist of pain inside her. Only was he going to stay around long enough for her to conceive? If she hadn't conceived already... Oh God. It would have been a great deal simpler if she hadn't fallen in love with him; if you didn't love, you couldn't be hurt, and she thought she was hurting very badly now. But how did you fight for a man who saw you only as a possession?

Forcibly reminding herself that it had been a week, hardly time for them to get to know each other, let alone write off the marriage, she turned her attention to the rubbish stacked in the loft. Crawling carefully over the old beams, she collected everything together. Breakable objects she carefully lowered, non-breakables she simply tossed down on to the landing.

Sorting out the wants from the don't wants into two piles, she carried all the junk downstairs and put it outside by the dustbin. Returning upstairs, she gathered up the rest and carried everything into her bedroom, where she dumped it on the bed. One box contained only broken toys, a chipped china bowl, and, for some odd reason, two spoons. Putting them to one side to be put out with the rubbish, Sam turned her attention to the box of books and papers. Some of the books were worth keeping, others were mildewed round the edges, and she put them with the rubbish pile. As she lifted out the remainder, one of the books slithered to the floor, and as she bent to retrieve it she saw it was the book Julie had had in the hospital—her record, as she'd called it, a little hardbacked book with a brass lock and key, except that the lock was broken, and there was no longer any key. Maybe when she could face it, Sam would read it; it might help others suffering from the disease—assuming that it was a record of Julie's illness.

As she opened it, intending only a quick perusal, a photograph fluttered out to lie face down on the carpet. Picking it up, she gave it an idle glance—then froze in shock. It could be one of Julie's relatives, she tried to persuade herself, an uncle or something, only she knew in her heart that it wasn't any such thing. It was Robbie to the life. Or as Robbie might be in twenty years' time. Staring down at the face that stared so indifferently back, Sam felt sick, hot, then cold.

Dark brown eyes stared out at her, the exact shape of Robbie's; dark hair fell across a broad forehead in exact replica of Robbie. Even the smile was a smile she saw every day. Turning it over, she read the name on the back, Lester Voight, and stamped at the bottom the name and address of the photographer.

Feeling cold and sick, she put it shakily to one side, and turned her attention to the book it had come from. Not a record of Julie's illness at all, and she wanted to bury it back in the box along with the photo, pretend she'd never seen it, only she couldn't.

Staring down at the first page, she picked nervously at a ragged nail. 'For Robbie,' she read, 'when he's old enough to understand, and forgive. And for Sam, who loved me enough to make the dying easier.'

Tears flooding into her eyes as she read the poignant words, Sam searched for a hanky. Blowing her nose hard, she took a deep breath and began flicking over the pages. At first her actions were automatic, fatalistic even, until a name leapt out at her. Devlin Howe.

An hour later, she closed the book with a soft snap, the photograph tucked back inside. She sat for a long time like that, thinking about all that she'd read, all the little puzzles that now became clear. She'd by no means read it properly, only really the bits that confirmed that Robbie was not Devlin Howe's son.

Poor Julie, she thought emptily. All those walks in the park, to think, to plan her life—or so she had told Sam, and which in reality had been nothing of the sort. They'd been walks to meet Lester Voight, who had been on a business course, down from the Midlands, and Julie had fallen in love with him, thought he'd fallen in love with her, otherwise she would never have gone back to his hotel room with him—otherwise she would never have let him make love to her. And then to find he was married—even to answer the phone to his wife...

With a long, shaky sigh, the book held limply in her lap, Sam stared down at it, not seeing it. It even explained the row with her mother. Julie must have come back from the hotel, before Sam had arrived home from work. Her mother had rung, and Julie, still upset, needing quiet, time to think, instead had had her mother harassing her... No wonder she had wanted to go down to the cottage a day early! It also explained why Julie had wanted the phone taken out. So that Lester couldn't keep ringing her; her mother couldn't keep ringing her. And now Lester lived in Germany, with his wife and three children. Did he know about Robbie? No, probably not. Sam didn't think Julie would have told him;

although presumably Lester must have written to her, otherwise Julie wouldn't have known he was in Germany. But it certainly explained why she had been upset enough to get drunk with Devlin—and to end up in his bed; but not to make love. Julie wrote that Devlin hadn't touched her; he had fallen asleep. They'd both been too drunk to do anything. Don't tell Devlin Robbie's his—because of course he wasn't.

A strong man, a good man, exciting, demanding, arrogant, lovable. But not Robbie's father. And not in love with herself. If he had been, they might have worked something out. But he wasn't. And if Sam had been listening with her mind instead of her emotions when he first came, wouldn't she have known he wasn't the father? Upset, Devlin had said about his first meeting with Julie, perhaps some man had dumped her. No, Sam had scoffed, there had been no other men. She'd been so sure, so arrogantly sure that she knew best.

She couldn't tell him. How could she? And swift on the heels of that thought, how could she not? She could burn the diary and the photograph—and if in the future Lester Voight, father of Robbie, turned up demanding to see his son, she could pretend ignorance, couldn't she? No. Yet if she told Devlin, there would be no talk, no trying to work it out—there would be nothing. Devlin would leave. She wouldn't see him again. And she didn't think she could bear that.

He need never know, her mind whispered. Who would it hurt? If this Lester Voight hadn't come by now, odds were that he never would. If he didn't know about Robbie, what good would it do to tell him? He was married, had a family of his own.

And if she tracked him down, told him, what if he suggested taking Robbie? Adopting him? No, Julie hadn't wanted that. Clamping down on the hysteria that was threatening, Sam tried to think. She had to tell Devlin. Why? Why did she? Because it was unfair not to. Unfair to whom? And then the front door slammed. Heavy footsteps echoed along the hall, halted at the bottom of the stairs.

'Sam?'

Incapable of answering, of doing anything except sit staring at the door, she heard his muttered imprecation, then the front room door open and close, the kitchen door, before heavy impatient steps returned to the stairs and began to ascend.

Without even thinking about it, she thrust the book back into the box and shoved the whole lot under the bed. Her heart racing, she knelt on the floor and began to gather up the books she had discarded to be thrown out.

'Sam? Where the hell are you? Didn't you hear me calling?' he demanded irritably as he halted in the bedroom doorway. Then his impatient expression gentled as he took in her white, tear-stained face. 'Sam?' he asked gently. 'What's wrong? Is it Robbie?'

Shaking her head, her eyes still holding shock, she gathered up the books and stood up. 'I have to throw these out,' she said jerkily.

'Julie's?' he guessed, and she just stared at him. Tell him! her mind screamed.

'Oh, Sam. It's only been three months, you're bound to be upset. Come on, put them away and come downstairs...'

'Don't be nice to me,' she whispered. 'You don't understand.'

'Well, of course I understand! You're upset! She was your friend——'

'No!' With a little sob, she pushed past him, barely able to see where she was going, and nearly fell down the stairs. Wrenching open the back door, she threw the old books on to the growing pile of rubbish. Tell him? she thought. I can't!

The rest of the day was a nightmare. Consumed by guilt, Sam mechanically carried out the tasks she normally did. She made some tea, but didn't drink it. She began preparations for dinner, then abandoned them.

'Sam! Will you for God's sake sit down? Listen to the radio, read a book——'

'I'm going out,' she said bluntly, staring at Devlin as though she'd never seen him before, her eyes wide and blank.

'Then go out!' he said impatiently. 'Only for heaven's sake get yourself together before Robbie comes home!'

'Yes.' Grabbing her coat and car keys, she went. Ran away. Coward, she thought. Go back and tell him. Now, before he finds out for himself. No. She'd tell him in the morning, when she was calmer, had thought it all through, worked out what to say. It was no good blurting it all out when she was upset. It would come out all wrong. And when she did tell him, he would leave. Pulling over to the side of the road, Sam rested her arms on the steering-wheel and began to cry.

When she eventually returned to the cottage, it was gone seven.

'I bathed Robbie and put him to bed,' Devlin informed her quietly. 'He's waiting for you to tuck him in. Feel better now?'

'Yes,' she whispered, 'thank you. I'm sorry I was so——'

'It's all right.'

Nodding, she went upstairs to see to Robbie. If he noticed her blotchy face and puffy eyes, he didn't say anything, just gave her a hug and turned over to sleep.

Tell him now, Sam. Just walk downstairs, and tell him.

'I'll get the dinner on, shall I?' she asked listlessly when she returned to the lounge.

'I'm not hungry. I think I'll go out for a pint, I'll get something later.'

'All right,' she agreed quietly. 'Devlin, I . . . I might have an early night.'

'Sure.' With a last searching glance at her, he walked out.

When he returned at just after ten, she was in bed. When he came up, she pretended to be asleep. He probably knew she wasn't but to her relief didn't comment, just undressed quietly in the dark, walked equally quietly along to the bathroom, then climbed into bed, to lie as far away from her as possible. Sam lay for a long time, silent tears trickling down her cheeks, staring at the wall, her back to him. He didn't sleep either, she could feel by the way he lay, the quiet, even breathing, not deep enough for sleep. She could tell him now, in the dark, when she wouldn't be able to see his face—and in the morning, he would leave.

CHAPTER SEVEN

WHEN Sam woke in the morning, Devlin was already up and dressed, and she lay for a few minutes staring blankly at nothing. She had to tell him now. No more putting it off. It wasn't fair. Devlin deserved better than that. She'd been selfishly only thinking of herself. He had courageously shouldered responsibilities he thought were his, and it was bitterly unfair of her to expect him to carry on doing so when he had no need. Fine words, she mocked herself.

Getting up, she quickly washed and dressed and went downstairs. Standing in the kitchen doorway, she stared at them—Devlin sitting opposite Robbie, explaining something to him, one of his toy cars in his large hands, a look of intense concentration on the boy's face as he listened. They liked each other, these two, had come to know and understand each other. How could she take it all away? Devlin had come to mean as much to her as Robbie did. More in some ways—and when she told him, he would leave. Thankfully? She didn't think she could bear that—to see relief on his strong face. Wouldn't it be quicker, cleaner, easier, if she told him he must go? Would the hurt be less?

'Feeling better?' Devlin asked quietly as he became aware of her silent figure.

'Yes.' Searching his face, looking, she supposed, for a trace of warmth, a suggestion of love, Sam gave a sad smile. 'Is there tea in the pot?'

When he nodded, she walked across to pour herself a cup, giving Robbie an affectionate squeeze on her way past him. When she was seated at the table, she searched Devlin's face again. 'We need to talk,' she said quietly.

'Yes, we do.' Turning to Robbie, he handed the car over. 'See if it works now, hm? Up on the landing will be the best place.'

'OK.' With a grin for Sam, Robbie went out and upstairs.

'You didn't sleep,' Devlin stated quietly.

'No, I had a lot on my mind. I'm sorry about yesterday...'

'It's all right, you were upset. You still look a bit white.'

'Yes.' We sound like strangers, she thought. How we were at the beginning. Staring down into her cup, she took a deep steadying breath. 'I...' Then she closed her eyes in defeat when she heard Robbie clattering back downstairs.

'Sam! Sam!' he yelled excitedly, erupting into the kitchen. 'Look what I found! Can I have it? Can I?'

With a sigh of defeat, she turned round—and froze. Robbie was holding Julie's book. 'Where did you find it?' she asked, her voice cracked and uneven.

'Under your bed.'

'And what were you doing in my room?'

'My car rolled in there,' he said indignantly. 'Can I have it?'

'No.' Thrusting her chair back, Devlin was quicker, and she stared at him numbly as he took the book from Robbie.

'Go back up and play,' he told the boy quietly, his eyes never leaving Sam's white face.

Knowing he could see the guilt and confusion in her eyes, she looked down. 'I...'

'Yes?' he asked coldly.

'It's a diary.'

'Is it? Would I find it interesting, Sam?'

'What?' Staring back at him, her guilt replaced by confusion, she wondered at the look of distaste on his face.

'Secret jottings, Sam?' Moving his eyes from hers, Devlin looked down and opened the book.

'No!' she exclaimed hoarsely, her hand outstretched as though to stop him, then she allowed her hand to drop limply to her side. 'It will be better if I tell you first, before you read it.'

'Oh, I'm sure it would. I'll take Robbie over to the Gunners'. We need to be on our own, I think.' Turning on his heel, he called Robbie, and Sam scrambled to her feet and followed him.

'I'll take him,' she insisted quietly.

'Yes, I thought you might.' Without looking at her, Devlin pushed into the lounge and shut the door.

Puzzled, Sam forced herself to smile at Robbie. 'Want to go back to play with Peter?'

'Yeah!' he said eagerly. 'Can I take my car?'

'Yes, of course.'

When she'd dropped him off with a bewildered Barbara, who after one look at Sam's white face insisted Robbie stay for the night, Sam began the drive back to the cottage, then changed her mind. Confused and worried by Devlin's reaction, she needed time to think, and also time for Devlin to read the book. It had almost been as though he'd known what to expect, as though he weren't surprised, yet he couldn't have seen the book before. Or could he? Secret jottings, he'd said. Would he find it interesting? Well, he surely would find it that. Although devastating might be a better word. Only the words didn't matter, did they? The end result would be the same: he would leave. And knowing that he must, she wanted it over quickly. She wouldn't be able to take long-drawn-out discussions, recriminations. So, to make it quick, she would tell him he must leave. Tell him, before he told her.

Turning the car, she set off back to the cottage, her face reflecting the false calm of desperation.

Devlin was waiting for her, as she had known he would be. He was sitting in the armchair by the fire, the diary open on his lap. His face held no expression whatsoever, but he couldn't hide the small nerve jumping in his jaw. He was angry, so very angry, she thought helplessly.

'Sit down,' he said peremptorily when she walked in. She sat. '"Don't tell Devlin it's his." Takes on a whole new meaning now, doesn't it, Sam? Because of course he wasn't mine.'

'No, he wasn't—isn't—yours,' she managed quietly.

'I didn't even touch her!' he yelled, leaping to his feet as though to sit still was more than he could bear. 'All this time, disgusted with myself for seducing her, for being drunk and not remembering—and I didn't even touch her!'

'No,' she whispered, her throat dry, her eyes fixed widely on his face, almost flinching from the anger that radiated from him. 'But I didn't know, Devlin, I truly didn't know.' Taking a deep breath, she plunged into the story she had mentally rehearsed while she'd been driving before she lost her courage. 'Fortunately we found out before too much damage has been done, before Robbie comes to rely on you. It will be best all round if we leave now, get packed up,' she babbled frantically in the face of his hard stare, the dangerously narrowed eyes. 'Barbara can probably put us up for a few days until we find somewhere...'

'Yes, you'd like that, wouldn't you, Sam?' he asked with quiet savagery. 'To run away without questions being asked. You had it all worked out from the very beginning, didn't you? The minute I walked through that door——'

'No!' she exclaimed in astonishment. 'How could I have done? I didn't know you! Didn't know you owned the cottage...'

'Didn't you?' he asked softly. Opening the book, riffling quickly through the pages until he came to the passage he wanted, he began to read. '"Paul came to see me today..."'

'Paul?' she queried blankly as she sank back into the chair.

'Yes, Sam, Paul. "He told me he wouldn't accept Robbie, that I was to tell Sam I no longer wanted her to look after him,"' he continued, slowly, reading carefully, explicitly, spitefully. '"I didn't like Paul, so I refused. I'm pleased Paul won't have the responsibility of my son, and Sam will be all right, when Devlin comes back, he won't turn her out. Despite his gruff exterior, he's a kind man." And I am, Sam, aren't I? Very kind—and gullible.' Returning his attention to the book, he continued harshly, '"Sam's very beautiful, perhaps——"'

'No!' she said again. Not in denial of her beauty, but denial for what Julie had seemed to be presuming. 'Devlin, I didn't know! I didn't find the book until yesterday!'

'Oh, I believe that part,' he said with awful sarcasm. 'That's why you were so shocked. Didn't know she'd written it all down, did you? You should have burnt it, then I might never have found out.'

'Don't be a fool! If I'd known you weren't his father I'd never have married you!'

'Wouldn't you?' he asked nastily.

'No! I only married you because of Robbie!' And unbelievably, he seemed to flinch, but before she could pursue his odd reaction he turned away and returned to his chair. When he faced her again, his face was harder if anything, his expression savage. The book held loosely in his hands, he continued with quiet emphasis, 'Funny, really. I thought you were just upset at having to go through her things. And then later, when David was here, I decided it wasn't perhaps entirely that.' With a half-laugh that wasn't in the least humorous, he added, 'I thought David had given you an ultimatum.' Returning his gaze to the book, he murmured almost to himself, 'I'd come to the conclusion that you'd only married me because you couldn't have David Gunner, and were determined to make the marriage work—only you discovered too late that your feelings for David were too strong to pretend. I thought that was why you'd been behaving so oddly. I was even prepared to try and overlook it. When we moved, I persuaded myself, you wouldn't be able to see him so easily. And then when Robbie found the book, and I saw your guilt, I was convinced of it. I thought it was your secret diary. Details of your assignations with Gunner—and that was why you didn't want me to see it. That was why you insisted on taking Robbie, to warn David that I'd found out. Only of course that was only part of it, wasn't it? Whatever your feelings for David might be, you intended to stay married to me, didn't you? Why?' he demanded.

Why? Because I fell in love with you, she thought achingly. Only he really wanted to know that, didn't he? she thought bleakly. 'I didn't want to stay married to you,' she lied. 'I told you, I only married you because of Robbie, it had nothing whatever to do with David.' Staring blankly at him, she couldn't believe he could think anything so stupid, and she shook her head in mute denial. Yet it made a crazy sort of sense, didn't it? All those things he'd said, if he believed she'd been having an affair with David. Poor David, he would be absolutely horrified if he knew.

'And that was the only reason?' Devlin asked, a sneer twisting his mouth.

'Yes. All those things you said were true, that Robbie needed a firm hand, discipline, and I also thought that if I denied him the right of being with his real father, as I thought you were, he would later resent me, hate me. I love Robbie, I wanted only what was best for him—you said it yourself. But now that we know you're not the father...'

'You can't wait to get rid of me, can you?' he asked bitterly. 'You used me! Julie used me! Planned it all, down to the last——'

'No! Devlin, she was dying! She wasn't rational, coldly calculating! Half the time she didn't even make sense——'

'This makes sense!' he shouted, slapping the book down on the armchair, making her jump.

'But she must have written that before the drugs made her confused...'

'Yes!' he hissed triumphantly, his face contorted. 'Which means you must have known! Even your insistence that I have tests was a calculated plan, wasn't it? Then when, if, I did ever find out, you could protest, with genuine truth, that you'd told me to make absolutely sure.'

'No!'

'Yes!' he insisted, leaping to his feet once more. 'A deliberate trap!' Slamming the book shut, he threw it into her lap. 'A souvenir of deceit,' he said scathingly. 'And right at this moment I'd like nothing better than to sling you out—only I can't, can I? Because of Robbie, because he's the other innocent dupe in all this, isn't he? So for his sake, I will allow you to stay in the cottage until it's sold. I will even instruct the agent that exchange of contracts must be after the date you're due to move back to your flat.'

'Thank you,' Sam said tonelessly. What else was there to say?

'Thank you,' he mimicked. With insulting thoroughness, he examined her from head to foot, then with a look of disgust he turned away and picked up the holdall he had left by the door. 'I've packed up all my things, items that I particularly wanted, and put them in the Range Rover. Anything that's left can be sold with the cottage—the agent has an inventory, just in case you were thinking of adding some furnishings to your flat. Goodbye, Sam. If you can't persuade David to leave his wife and join you, perhaps you can persuade

Paul to take you back—or find another sucker. A divorce shouldn't present too many problems—after all, I have grounds, don't I? Don't I, Sam?'

'Yes,' she agreed quietly. 'Goodbye, Devlin.' The hard slam of the door was her answer.

She sat there for a long time after he had gone. Just sat there, shaking. Hating herself, hating Julie. His accusations explained so many things about his behaviour the last few days. Or had he only believed it because that was what he wanted to believe? Because it made it easier for him to go? Thinking about that, instead of her own hurt, she frowned. Did he really believe she and David were having a clandestine affair? Or had he too been planning some convenient escape route if the marriage didn't work out? He'd certainly twisted everything he'd read in the diary to suit himself, she thought slowly as she recalled the things he'd said. Disbelieving her protests utterly—and that made her angry. She could, she thought, have accepted it had he genuinely believed her guilty; but if it had been merely an excuse to account for his own behaviour, then that was cowardly. In fact the more she thought about it, the angrier she became, finally convincing herself that she was right. And why, why should it all matter to him so much? He'd been the one to force marriage! She hadn't insisted, hinted, hadn't done any damned thing except comply with his dictates! And he'd said himself it was for Robbie's own sake! No, he was using the book as an excuse to leave, she was convinced of it. He'd had a moment of chivalry, an unaccustomed twinge of conscience, and come back from Spain! Had he expected her to put up more of a fight against the wedding? And when she hadn't, had he gone through with it in a fit of defiance?

Sitting in the chair, Sam turned it over and over in her mind, trying to view it from all angles—and came to the conclusion that she was right. That Devlin had deliberately interpreted the facts to suit himself as an excuse to leave, to cover up his own feelings, or lack of them. That he couldn't be man enough to admit to his own mistakes. In fact everything that had happened had happened as a direct result of his own arrogance. *He'd* believed he'd been the father! *He'd* insisted they get married! *He'd* been the one who denied the necessity of taking any tests! And then he'd arrogantly blamed her for all his shortcomings. Well, to hell with him! They didn't need him! They'd got on fine before he came, and would now he'd gone!

Storming around the cottage, clearing up the kitchen, Hoovering the lounge, Sam suddenly remembered what he'd said about Paul going to see Julie. Oh, wasn't anyone ever as they seemed? Devlin, Julie, Paul. Going back to the lounge, she retrieved the book from the chair and sat down to read it properly. When she had finished, she slowly closed it. Oh, Julie, didn't I know you at all? she thought. If she'd told her that Paul had been to see her at least Sam would have been prepared, not have had to go through all that mental anguish. And to deliberately engineer a meeting with Devlin... She would have sworn with her dying breath that Julie hadn't had a devious bone in her body—and she'd have been wrong.

Feeling cheated and disillusioned, unable to sit still, she dragged herself upstairs to make the beds. Automatically folding things and shoving them into

the drawer, she came across one of Devlin's
sweaters, and all her feelings of ill-usage came tum-
bling back. Dragging it out, she flung it at the wall.
Bastard! How dared he treat her like a no-account-
nothing? She'd given her love to him! The fact that
he didn't know she had had nothing whatever to
do with it! She'd given it and he'd thrown it back
in her face! Anger and frustration churning away
inside her, she stalked round the cottage like a caged
tiger, muttering to herself, calling him all the names
she could think of.

Exhausted, angry, unable to rest, unable to think
straight, she eventually went to bed, only to lie
awake, going all over it again and again. She didn't
sleep, she knew she didn't, and after watching the
clock ticking round for what seemed like hours she
got up and made herself some tea. Hateful, un-
merciless, cheating—— In fury, she hurled her cup
at the wall. Well, she was damned if she was going
to be the fall guy, the patsy! If he thought he could
get away with that he was mistaken! She couldn't
take it out on Julie. Julie was beyond reach. Or
Paul, another lying, cheating bastard. But Devlin
wasn't beyond her reach, beyond her tongue! Oh,
no! Thrusting back her chair, Sam ran upstairs to
dress. Seeing Devlin's offending sweater, still on the
floor where she'd hurled it, she grabbed it and
hurried down again. Shrugging into her coat,
thrusting her feet into shoes, she snatched her car
keys from the mantelpiece and went out. It was still
dark, barely six o'clock, she saw with surprise from
the dashboard clock. Well, who cared? If he was
in bed, she would get him up! If she couldn't sleep,
why the hell should he?

Whipping up her anger as she drove far too fast towards Hastings, dredging up all the real and imagined slights she had received from Devlin since the day he had walked in through the cottage door, she arrived at the house in a mood of downright fury. Her hair a tangled mess, her eyes brightly green, she hammered on his door.

When nothing happened, she hammered on it again, then gave it a kick for good measure. When a light finally came on inside, and the door slowly opened, she glared at the dishevelled figure revealed.

He took one horrified look at her face and tried to slam the door.

Horrified? Sam thought blankly. Why should he be horrified? Snapping back to the reason for her visit, she gave the door a hearty shove and stormed into the hall. 'Don't you dare slam the door in my face! I want to talk to you,' she told him aggressively. Thrusting the door closed, she stared at him. He looked a mess—unshaven, his hair sticking out all over the place, eyes red-rimmed, and wearing only his short navy bathrobe. 'You look terrible!'

'Thank you. And what the hell did you expect, getting me up in the middle of the night?'

'It's not the middle of the night! It's half-past six,' she informed him coldly without looking at her watch.

'Half-past six?' he exclaimed incredulously. 'Oh, for God's sake, I'm going back to bed.'

'No, you aren't. Are you ill?'

'Ill?' he queried blankly, his eyes only seeming to be half focused on her face. 'No, of course I'm not ill! I'm never ill! And I wish you'd go away!' Smothering a wide yawn, he leaned, or, more correctly, fell against the wall and continued to regard her with unconcealed dislike. 'I'm drunk. All right? Does that make you feel better?'

'No. And why are you drunk at this time in the morning?'

'Why?' he exclaimed wrathfully. 'Why? Because I polished off a bottle of Scotch last night, that's why!'

Giving him a look of disgust, Sam stormed past him into the kitchen. None of this was going as she'd planned, she thought furiously. Why the hell did he have to be drunk? And why did he have to look so damned vulnerable? He was never vulnerable! Plonking his sweater on the table, she went to put the kettle on. Finding cups and the coffee and sugar, she ignored him as he blundered in behind her and collapsed at the table.

'Do you have to make so much noise?' he complained irritably. 'I've got the mother and father of all headaches.'

'I'm not surprised,' she retorted unsympathetically. 'And you didn't tell me why you're drunk.'

'Was,' he muttered, accepting his coffee and burying his nose in it. 'Was drunk—now I'm hung over.'

'All right, why were you drunk?' she asked with heavy patience.

'Why are you here?' he parried without looking at her. 'And what the hell's this?' he asked, poking suspiciously at the mound of grey wool.

'One of your sweaters. I thought you might like it back!'

'How kind,' he approved sarcastically. 'Washed and ironed, is it?'

'No, it isn't! And you're lucky I didn't burn it, the way I feel! You accused me of all sorts of things without foundation——'

'Without foundation?' he expostulated, his eyebrows almost climbing into his hair. 'Without—'

'Shut up! You took a lot of facts, half-facts and suppositions and made them into a case to suit yourself! And how dared you accuse me of plotting with Julie?'

'Dare? Dare?' he shouted. 'You practically admitted it!'

'I did no such thing! And whether I admitted it or not,' she contradicted herself, 'you had no right to accuse me! If you wanted to know anything you only had to ask!'

'I did ask!'

'No, you didn't! And then—then you accused me of trapping you! Of selling myself!'

'I did not!'

'Yes, you did!' she screamed. 'How dare you blame your own shortcomings on me?'

'My what?' he demanded, slamming his cup down so that hot coffee slopped all over his hand. 'Ouch!' Hastily sucking the side of his hand, he glared at her.

'Shortcomings! Suspicion, jealousy——'

'I was not jealous!'

'All right, possessive! God knows why you should get it into your thick head that David and I were having an affair, but let me tell you it was as far from the truth as Tinkerbell having an affair with—with the Elephant Man! My God, he'd have been horrified if he'd known what you thought! He loves his wife! He's devoted to her!'

'And you, Sam?' Devlin asked nastily, sitting down again. 'Are you devoted to her?'

'Yes!' she gritted. 'And to David! As friends!'

'Hah! Think I'm blind? That I didn't see the soft little smiles you gave him? The whispering at Christmas——'

'We were whispering,' she said through her teeth, 'because he didn't want you to hear what present he'd bought you!'

'Oh, well, there you are, then! And I suppose you're now about to tell me that you kissed him with such enthusiasm because he'd bought me a present!'

'I kissed him because it was Christmas! Because he likes me! Because we're friends!'

'He kissed you by your express invitation with all the coy looks you were giving him!' he contradicted violently.

'Coy?' she yelled, incensed. 'I've never been coy in my life!'

'Don't shout!' he roared, then moaned in pain and held his head. 'Ahh!'

'Don't be such a baby,' Sam said more moderately. And how the hell could you have a blazing row with someone who had a hangover? It was ludicrous. And frustrating. She needed to have a blazing row with him! 'Don't you have any aspirin?'

'No.'

'Then drink your coffee.'

'I'd rather go back to bed.'

'Well, you can't, not until you've listened to what I have to say.'

'That's what I was afraid of,' he muttered picking up his cup again and beginning to sip noisily.

'Do you have to do that?'

'Yes.'

Glaring at him, she found she wanted to hit him. No, not just hit him, pulverise him, wallop and wallop him until he . . . Until he what? Gave in? He was behaving totally out of character, drunk or not. He never behaved in this flippant manner. Anger, yes, aggression, sarcasm, mockery, but not flippancy. Frowning, she stared at him, tried to puzzle it out. 'I didn't know about you, about Julie and Lester,' she said quietly. 'I genuinely thought you were Robbie's father——'

'Have you told him?' he broke in. 'That I'm not?'

'No,' she denied crossly. 'How could I tell him? I haven't seen him since yesterday.'

'Then I suggest you go and tell him.' Slamming his cup down again, he shoved his chair back and got to his feet. 'Like now.'

He took one step away from the table, then yelped in pain. Grabbing the chair back, he shut his eyes tight and swallowed hard.

'What?' she yelled leaping to her feet, her eyes wide with worry—then she stared down in horrified fascination at the blood slowly dripping from one raised foot. 'Oh, my God!' she exclaimed faintly.

'Helpful,' he muttered. 'Well, don't just stand there with your mouth open—get me something to stop it bleeding.'

With a look of exasperation, she grabbed the roll of kitchen towel and thrust it at him.

'Well, tear a piece off!' he said impatiently. 'I can't do it one-handed, can I?'

'Then sit down.'

Giving her a look of disgust, Devlin collapsed back in his chair and raised his injured foot to rest on his other knee. Wadding up some tissue, he held it to the ball of his foot. 'Well, that will teach me to make grand exits, won't it?'

'Or it might teach you to watch where you're putting your feet!' Sam contradicted waspishly. 'Do you have a medicine cabinet?'

'No.'

'Well, what did you cut it on?'

'Your tongue, I wouldn't wonder.'

'Ha, ha.' Glancing down at the floor, Sam saw the piece of glass responsible and bent to pick it up. 'Where did this come from?'

The blood-soaked pad still held to one foot, his other arm resting on the table, his head propped in his palm, he regarded her with derision. 'Where do you think it came from? A passing space-ship? It came from a glass, Sam, a glass I broke last night.'

'Then why didn't you sweep it up?'

'Because, dear lady, I could barely see the floor, let alone a broken glass, and I was most certainly in no fit state to sweep it up. All right? Satisfied?'

'No. Why were you drunk?'

'Because some bloody stupid woman, whom I happened to quite like, took me for a ride! Played me for a fool! Happy now?' he asked sarcastically. 'Got all the mileage you wanted from it, have you?'

'No—and I didn't play you for a fool...'

'Did I say I was talking about you?'

'No, but it's a little hard to believe that there are two women around who could be so accused all in the space of a week. Isn't it?'

Scowling at her, Devlin returned his attention to his foot. 'It's still bleeding,' he muttered peevishly.

With a heavy sigh, Sam got to her feet and tore off another wad of kitchen towel. Dampening it at the sink, she went over to him, removed his hand and replaced the wad he was using with her own. 'Hold that there.' Taking the used waste, she threw it in the bin.

'It probably needs stitching.'

'Probably,' she agreed, resuming her seat.

When he flicked his eyes up to hers, she saw a little gleam of amusement, hastily veiled, and her lips twitched. 'Did you really believe all those things you said?'

'I might.'

'Devlin!'

Glancing at her from the corner of his eyes, he pursed his lips thoughtfully for a moment. 'I did when I said them.'

'And now?'

'I don't know. I've had time to think since then. Hell, Sam, it was a shock! You'd had a day and a night to come to terms with it, I had barely an hour to read and digest it all. I felt—humiliated,' he mumbled.

'Humiliated?' she asked, puzzled. 'But why?'

'I don't know,' Devlin said evasively as he made a great production of dabbing at his foot.

'Yes, you do. Tell me—please, Devlin.'

With a long sigh, he leaned back. 'Julie seemed to think I'd automatically want to take on the role of husband and father for the simple reason that she wanted a secure home for her son. You only married me because of him——'

'But that was what you wanted! That was your argument, not mine!'

'I know, I know,' he muttered irritably. 'But I didn't know that then, did I? Didn't know I was being manipulated. I thought it had all come about by accident, I'd told myself that marrying you was the Grand Gesture—the ultimate sacrifice, noble and brave.'

Pulling his mouth into a derisive twist, he looked up at her. 'Self-deception is the worst deceit of all, Sam. Robbie was my son, or I thought he was. He didn't deserve my indifference. That's what I told myself. Sitting here last night, I did a bit of soul-searching—with the aid of a bottle—and I wondered, if you'd been plain, frumpy, would I have offered marriage? No, of course I wouldn't. So where was the sacrifice? If you'd been unattractive, I'd have made financial provision and hightailed it out of there. I didn't even know why I cared about the looks you gave David. Oh, I told myself it was pique, that you preferred him to me, only of course it wasn't.' With a funny little shrug, he continued, 'I'd made my Grand Gesture and no one seemed to appreciate it. Can you believe that, Sam? A grown man behaving like a sulky child. I wanted praise, to be thanked—God, how pathetic! And then last night, I got to thinking, why was I so angry anyway? Why did it matter? If I didn't care for you, had no real feeling for Robbie, I should have been relieved to be rid of the responsibility. Only I wasn't,' he added quietly, staring back at his foot. 'I wanted you back. I wanted Robbie to be my son, I wanted him to like me.'

'He does like you,' she said softly.

'Yes, well...' When she didn't comment further, he looked up with a crooked smile, 'I'm a slow learner, Sam. I wouldn't admit to myself that you were right, about feelings. A good sex life, mutual liking, respect, they'd be enough. Only of course they weren't. And the smiles you gave David, that you didn't give to me, I thought—well, you know what I thought. It all seemed to fit. I didn't know how you felt about me, about the marriage. I had, after all, rushed you into it, and you have to admit you were behaving very oddly. Then when I read Julie's book, I discovered the feelings too late. You'd married me, as I thought, for financial security, because Julie thought it would be best for her son, or as a shield for your affair with David. Your denial, but admission that you'd only married me for Robbie's sake, was hardly guaranteed to make me feel good, was it? And as soon as you found out the truth, it was goodbye, Devlin, your services are no longer required. You expected me to leave. It is what you expected, isn't it, Sam?'

'Yes,' she whispered, her eyes lowered as she began to describe absent circles on the table-top. 'It's what I expected. But not what I wanted. That's why I was so upset. I didn't want you to go.'

'But you told me to——'

'To get in first, before you told me,' she explained quietly. 'To make the parting quicker. I thought you'd be relieved, you see, want to get out as soon as you could. Why should you want to stay? You didn't love me, care for me. Did you?'

'Cared for you, yes. Love? No, I didn't believe the state existed. But if loving is worrying about someone, caring what happens to them, wanting to kill the man who receives the smiles that I didn't get . . . If it means wanting to be held in the night— why did you want me to stay, Sam? What was it you wanted?'

Flicking her eyes up to his and then down again, Sam continued to draw her circles. He hadn't actually said he loved her. Not in so many words, had he? Yet she could no longer keep her own knowledge to herself. It was time for the truth. With a snatched little breath to give her courage, she clasped her hands in her lap and looked at him. 'For you to love me,' she confessed.

Holding her eyes, his own serious, intent, he asked softly, with barely a thread of sound, 'Why?'

'Because I loved you. Because it hurt not being loved in return. Because I wanted to tell you, and couldn't.'

'Ah, Sam!' he exclaimed on a long sigh. A small, gentle smile on his mouth, his eyes wryly amused, he reached across the table for her hand. 'So what do you do? You come knocking on my door at some unearthly hour, looking and acting like one of the Furies. I'm hung over, looking like death—and I wanted to strangle you. I had it all worked out, you see. I would get up, shower, shave, dress in my best bib and tucker, go and get the biggest bunch of red roses I could find, and come and beg you to take me back. Will you?'

'Yes,' she said simply.

'And let me be a father to Robbie? I do love him, Sam.'

'Yes,' she said again, and a slow smile spread across his face. With dark stubble shadowing his jaw, shadows beneath his red-rimmed eyes, his hair all over the place, it was the most beautiful smile she'd ever seen. Smiling shakily back, she squeezed his fingers.

'Aren't you sitting just the teeniest bit too far away?' he asked gently.

'Yes.' Getting to her feet, her knees feeling decidedly weak, Sam walked to stand in front of him, her hand still held in his. 'You look terrible,' she said softly.

'I feel terrible,' he admitted on a soft laugh, 'and I've never felt happier.'

Staring down at him, she put out her other hand to smooth down his hair, then allowed it to linger against his cheek. 'You need a shave.'

'And a shower, and to clean my teeth...'

'And have your foot seen to. There's a first-aid box in my car. I'll go and get you a plaster.'

His eyes crinkling with amusement, Devlin moved her hand to his mouth and kissed the palm. 'I'll go up and make myself presentable. Will you bring the plaster up to me?'

Nodding, finding suddenly that her throat was too dry to speak as a delicious warmth spread through her, Sam released her hand and went out to her car.

Returning a few minutes later with the box of plasters, she trod quietly up the stairs, following the sound of running water. Despite the steam misting the glass shower door, she could see Devlin's outline quite clearly. Leaning in the doorway, she watched him hungrily. When he turned the shower off and stepped out, she remained where she was, her eyes fixed on him, and he halted, staring at her, his eyes wide and steady on hers.

'Oh, Sam!' he exclaimed helplessly. 'You look—yearning.'

'Yes,' she whispered.

Closing his eyes, he took a deep shuddering breath, his hand gripping the towel at his side. Water ran slowly down his face from his wet hair, the cords in his neck stood proud as he forced himself under control. With another deep breath, he opened his eyes and quickly knotted the towel round his hips. 'Just let me shave,' he said thickly as he walked across to the sink.

When she didn't move or answer, he clasped his hands on the edge of the pale green porcelain, his head bowed. 'Don't watch me, Sam,' he groaned. 'Please.'

As she turned away, she saw the trail of bloody footprints, and only then remembered the plasters clasped in her hand. 'Best put a plaster on first,' she managed. 'I'll leave them on the edge of the bath.' Walking across, she left the box and quietly retreated.

Going into the bedroom next to the bathroom, she stood at the window, her hands clasped tightly in front of her. There could have been a herd of buffalo outside for all the notice she took of what she was seeing. Her vision, her thoughts were all on Devlin. On his strong, tanned body that would shortly be tangled with hers. On the play of muscles in his back as he'd leaned over the sink. The strong thighs. With a little groan, she clasped her hands across her waist as her stomach gave an alarming dip. Trying desperately to regulate her breathing, she didn't hear Devlin come in.

'Sam?'

Whirling round, she stared at him, her eyes wide, the blood thundering in her ears. For a moment, she was frightened by the intensity of her feelings, the awful ache lodged inside. Devlin was again wearing his navy robe, his hands pushed into the front pockets. He looked like a man under an unbearable strain.

'Hello,' she said foolishly, and he smiled.

'Hello.' Taking his hands from his pockets, he held his arms wide.

With a little cry, she ran into them, held him tight, her face buried against his chest. 'Oh, Devlin!'

'Oh, Sam,' he mocked gently, but his voice didn't seem any steadier than hers. 'What time do you have to pick Robbie up?'

'I don't know. But not yet,' she whispered.

'Good.' His arms tightening, he lowered his head until his mouth was against her thick, shining hair. 'I want to make love to you, Sam. Not sex, desire, want, or need. But love, with words, with feelings.'

'Yes.' Moving her head back, she looked up at him, her beautiful face shining with love. 'Yes,' she repeated. 'With love.'

Bending his head, he kissed her gently, reverently almost.

'Oh, Devlin, love me now!'

Swinging her up into his arms, he carried her out and into his own room, where he undressed her with exquisite tenderness, and when she was naked he shrugged out of his robe and drew her against him. 'One advantage of not having near neighbours,' he said softly, 'there's no need to draw the curtains.' Smiling down at her, he bent to capture her mouth with his.

HISTORICAL

CHRISTMAS

STORIES·1991

Bring back heartwarming memories of Christmas past,
with Historical Christmas Stories 1991, a collection of
romantic stories by three popular authors:

**Christmas Yet To Come
by Lynda Trent**

**A Season of Joy
by Caryn Cameron**

**Fortune's Gift
by DeLoras Scott**

A perfect Christmas gift!

HARLEQUIN

Romance

A Christmas tradition...

Imagine spending Christmas in New Orleans with a blind stranger and his aged guide dog—when you're supposed to be there on your honeymoon!
#3163 Every Kind of Heaven
by Bethany Campbell

Imagine spending Christmas with a man you once "married"—in a mock ceremony at the age of eight!
#3166 The Forgetful Bride
by Debbie Macomber

Available in December 1991, wherever Harlequin books are sold.

HARLEQUIN
PROUDLY PRESENTS
A DAZZLING NEW CONCEPT IN ROMANCE FICTION

One small town—twelve terrific love stories

Welcome to Tyler, Wisconsin—a town full of people
you'll enjoy getting to know, memorable friends and
unforgettable lovers, and a long-buried secret that
lurks beneath its serene surface....

JOIN US FOR A YEAR IN THE LIFE OF TYLER

Each book set in Tyler is a self-contained love story;
together, the twelve novels stitch the fabric of a
community.

LOSE YOUR HEART TO TYLER!

The excitement begins in March 1992, with
WHIRLWIND, by Nancy Martin. When lively, brash
Liza Baron arrives home unexpectedly, she moves
into the old family lodge, where the silent and
mysterious Cliff Forrester has been living in seclusion
for years....

WATCH FOR ALL TWELVE BOOKS
OF THE TYLER SERIES
Available wherever Harlequin books are sold

Take 4 bestselling love stories FREE

Plus get a FREE surprise gift!